BLOOD IN THE WATER

by Angela Roquet

Blood Vice
Blood Vice
Blood and Thunder
Blood in the Water
Blood Dolls
Thicker Than Blood
Blood, Sweat, and Tears
Flesh and Blood
Out for Blood

Lana Harvey, Reapers Inc.
Graveyard Shift
Pocket Full of Posies
For the Birds
Psychopomp
Death Wish
Ghost Market
Hellfire and Brimstone
Limbo City Lights (short story collection)
The Illustrated Guide to Limbo City

Spero Heights
Blood Moon
Death at First Sight
The Midnight District

Haunted Properties: Magic and Mayhem Universe
How to Sell a Haunted House
Better Haunts and Graveyards

other titles
Crazy Ex-Ghoulfriend
Backwoods Armageddon

BLOOD IN THE WATER

BLOOD VICE BOOK THREE

ANGELA ROQUET

VIOLENT SIREN PRESS

BLOOD IN THE WATER

www.angelaroquet.com

Cover Art by Rebecca Frank

Edited by Chelle Olson of Literally Addicted to Detail

ISBN: 978-1-951603-11-3

For Paul and Xavier,

who make my world go round.

Chapter One

The formal admission letter for the Blood Authority Training Center in Denver was vague as hell. I had no idea what to pack, and my frayed nerves weren't helping. Dialing up my diva sister in Hollywood to ask for advice probably hadn't been the best idea either.

"Don't forget moisturizer," Laura snapped. "That altitude is horrible for your skin. Oh! What about a bathing suit?"

"It's boot camp for vamps, not a vacation," I said.

"Hey, they might want you to do some swimming exercises. You never know."

I snorted and cradled my cell phone between my ear and shoulder so I could rummage through my duffel bag. So far, I was working with underwear, socks, and basic toiletries. The police academy had provided a dress code and gear list. Without that, I had no idea what was expected—and I certainly wasn't going to call Roman to find out.

Laura sighed in my ear. "Dumb question, but I'll ask it anyway. You're bringing blackout curtains for the hotel you stop at halfway, right?"

"Of course," I said a little too quickly, my voice hitching an octave.

"Don't *even* think about asking Max to drive all the way through."

"I won't."

"That's stupid dangerous," she went on, ignoring me entirely. "If you get into an accident—hell, if you're involved in a fender bender—you're up in flames."

"I said I won't, okay?" I huffed and snatched a pen and notepad off my night table, scribbling *curtains* down on the packing list.

Above the curtains, Mandy's chicken scratch detailed a dozen junk food items she'd insisted were essential to any proper road trip. And above that, Collins' typewriter-perfect print nailed down most of the important stuff: jumper cables, flares, flashlights with fresh batteries, survival blankets, extra water, a bag of oranges, pop-top beans, iron supplements, and a first aid kit. I was betting Collins had already gathered most of this stuff. And he'd probably packed his bags a week ago. At least one of us had it together.

"How's filming?" I asked Laura. Her heavy sigh almost made me regret changing the subject.

"David hired a writer from one of the teenybopper shows. I feel like I've been recast as a grandmother."

I smirked, feeling slightly smug that I had at least *one* thing going for me that Laura was jealous of. Eternal youth. In twenty years, she'd be touching up grays and getting Botox. Of course, I couldn't allow myself to think any further ahead than that. It was too depressing.

"And I don't have a single sex scene this season," Laura continued. She prattled on about the crappy set lighting and the heavy-handed makeup department, while I packed yoga pants and tank tops. I added a few long-sleeved tee shirts, wondering if any of this training would take place outside.

"So," I said once Laura ran out of things to complain about. "Are you still happy that you moved back?"

She huffed. "Yes. The constant sunshine, beaches, and adoring fans make all this crap worthwhile, I suppose. But I do miss you. Mandy even," she added.

I grinned. "We miss you, too."

We said our goodbyes, and I went to fish my bathing suit out of the back of my closet. Maybe Laura was right about the swimming exercises. Her guess was as good as mine.

As I hauled my packed duffel bag into the living room, the doorbell rang. Mandy had left earlier to say goodbye to Serena, but she had a key now. And Collins had a romantic evening planned with his husband for our last night in the city. Vin's shift at the morgue wasn't over for a few hours either. I was out of guesses.

My hand went to the holster at my hip, fingers curling around the grip of my Glock as I neared the front door. After the break-in a few weeks ago, I never went anywhere unarmed—not even within my own home.

I held my breath as I glanced through the peephole on

the front door. Roman Knight stood under the pale glow of the porch light. If not for his alarmingly blue eyes and white hair, I would have second-guessed his presence. He was in jeans and a gray, button-down shirt. His civilian clothes, I realized.

The last time I'd seen Roman had been at the Duke of House Lilith's manor in Ladue. That had been a few weeks ago, but it felt like ages. I'd expected him to visit or call me afterward, but when he hadn't, I suspected he was brooding over the duke admitting my blood harem and me into the training program.

The shame and wounded pride I felt from our most recent mishap had kept me from reaching out to him. I'd saved his life with my blood. That he'd been ungrateful was a massive understatement.

The way Roman saw it, I had deprived him of the opportunity to become a vampire fifty years sooner than his contract with Blood Vice stated. I'd strangled him within the one loophole he was allowed. And he hated me for it—a devastating blow to the torch I carried for him.

If that weren't enough to fuel my guilt, Roman had also put his career on the line to keep me from being sentenced to death by the very authority I was prepared to train with. That secret had the potential to end us both now.

I knew he had hoped I would be easy to sweep under the

rug. That I'd be some quiet, good deed he could pat himself on the back for whenever he was forced to slay some other sireless vampling on the duke's orders. I guess I was just too ambitious to go gentle into that good night.

The corners of Roman's mouth drew down as he impatiently pushed the doorbell again, and I noticed a briefcase in his opposite hand. I released my held breath and unlocked the door, pulling it open as if ripping off a bandage.

We stood there, staring at each other in silence for a long moment. I didn't know what to say to him, and he was clearly struggling to find words, too.

"Can I come in?" he finally asked.

I nodded stiffly and took a step back, opening a path for him. Roman pressed his lips together and took a deep breath through his nose before crossing my threshold, his shoulders squared and chin held high. I watched his throat bob as I closed the door behind him.

The living room felt too casual and intimate, especially with Mandy's half-folded basket of laundry strewn over the sofa, so I led Roman into the kitchen instead. I waved a hand at the stools along the breakfast bar, silently offering him a seat before circling the counter and facing him from the opposite side. The buffer seemed to put us both more at ease.

"What's the occasion?" I asked, pushing my tangle of blond hair over my shoulder. Roman's eyes dropped to my chest, and I remembered that I was still wearing the lace-trimmed tank top I'd worn to bed. Sans bra. I folded my arms over my breasts as his eyes darted down to my bare legs stretched out beneath a pair of cotton shorts. My skin flushed at the attention.

Roman set his briefcase on the countertop. His thumbs made short work of the combination lock, and the leather box sprang open, revealing several manila envelopes. He removed them and dug a fingernail under the dark lining along the bottom of the case. A hidden compartment popped open, and from it, he retrieved a tiny, plastic box containing a micro SD card.

"Is your cell phone password protected? Are you able to listen to classified files on it?" he asked, sliding the box with the chip across the counter toward me.

I frowned but gave him a quick nod. "What is this?"

Roman took another deep breath and blinked up at me. I wondered how long he had been dreading this meeting.

"Can you tell me your sire's name?" he asked flatly.

I felt my cheeks warm, even though I'd been practicing. "Pablo Zajalvo," I answered.

"And what do you know about him?"

"He immigrated to the States from Spain ten years ago."

Roman raised an eyebrow. "What's the name of his village in Spain?"

"You never told me." I refrained from snorting at him. "Is that what's on this chip?"

"Among other things." Roman looked away from me as he tucked the manila folders back inside his briefcase. "You're not ready for Blood Vice. Not by a long shot." He scoffed, but the sound was more disappointed than patronizing. "I wasn't able to talk any sense into you before. That chip is all the help I have to offer on such short notice."

"Thank you." I wasn't about to look a gift horse in the mouth, especially since I hadn't expected Roman to come bearing gifts in the first place.

He cleared his throat and rolled a thumb over the dials on the case, locking it. "When do you leave?" he asked.

"Tomorrow evening, as soon as I rise."

Roman nodded and cleared his throat again before tugging at the cuffs of his shirt. He couldn't seem to make eye contact with me for more than a second or two. It was unnerving, and I wasn't sure if his discomfort stemmed from guilt—like my own uneasiness—or from something else.

Sharing blood was disconcertingly invasive. Like walking in on someone while they were naked. Or bumping into them and grazing their crotch with your hand. It was awkward and sometimes unintentionally intimate, especially in a life-or-death situation. I remembered the conflicted feelings I'd had after Roman saved my life…and now I imagined he was riding that same roller coaster.

"Any final words of wisdom?" I asked, trying to fill the looming silence.

"Don't share anything with anyone that you don't have to," he said. "Don't try to make friends."

I narrowed my eyes at him. "Is that advice working out well for you?"

"I'm serious." A muscle in his jaw feathered, and his gaze met mine. "The other cadets will be more experienced and conniving. They'll use anything you give them to gain an advantage. This isn't like the police academy, Jenna. And it's no Quantico either. The bat cave might sound like a cute nickname, but I assure you, it's like nothing you've experienced. Be careful."

I swallowed a scathing remark and nodded, trying to push past the tension to find some sliver of gratitude. Roman was trying to help. He didn't have to. I could cut him some slack for his effort—even if it was at least half-inspired by self-preservation.

"I'll be careful," I said. "Thanks." I held up the plastic box with the memory card.

"Don't mention it. To anyone," he added, confirming the literal sense of his reply.

Roman pulled the briefcase off the counter and turned for the living room. I followed him to the front door, keeping a comfortable distance between us. His cocoa butter and grass scent tended to overwhelm me whenever I got too close, and I wondered what he would smell like once fall and winter set in. It was ridiculous, but I was looking forward to finding out once I returned from Denver.

Out on my front porch, Roman turned to face me. "There's a bed and breakfast halfway between here and Denver," he said, blanching as if he weren't really sure he wanted to share the information. "It's just past Salina, Kansas. They cater to your kind. The Cottage Crypt." At my raised eyebrow he added, "Vanessa and I stayed there on our way to St. Louis."

"I'll check it out."

Roman dipped his head in a final farewell nod before descending the porch steps and cutting across the dark lawn toward his SUV. As I watched him pull away from the curb, I tugged my cell phone out of the waistband of my shorts, eager to investigate what was on the chip.

Hopefully, something more useful than a bathing suit or jumper cables.

"Ouch!" I jerked my arm away from Vin and grimaced as I rubbed the angry welt forming in the bend of my elbow.

"Just because I heal faster, doesn't mean that hurts any less," I snapped, leaning away as Vin reached for me.

"Sorry." He bit his bottom lip and gave me a pained smile. "Your quick healing is part of the problem. I have to push the needle in deeper just to keep the blood flowing long enough to fill one of these." He pushed his glasses up the bridge of his nose and shook a tube of my dark blood before slipping it inside an insulated lunch bag where he'd stashed five more just like it.

In the past, he'd drawn two at most. But since I would be in Denver for the next three months, he'd requested more. My conscience was taking a beating for it—along with my elbows.

Once I became an official Blood Vice agent, I would be expected to arrest vampires who supplied human doctors or scientists with their blood for study and experimentation. I felt like a total hypocrite, and I knew that this part of my relationship with Vin would have to come to an end soon.

I should have cut him off a long time ago, but I'd let guilt cripple my morals. Guilt over the fact that I couldn't offer him a normal relationship. We would never have a nice meal together. Never share a bag of popcorn at the movies or have Christmas dinner with his family. We'd never feed each other wedding cake. We'd never have children. We would never grow old together.

This thing we had was dying, and there was no preventing it. And while he was *technically* part of my blood harem, he was outside the inner circle. He wasn't going with us to Denver. Vin was a forensic pathologist at the county morgue. He couldn't just take a three-month vacation to follow me across the country because I *vanted to suck his blood.* If I were being honest with myself, it wasn't really *his* blood I *vanted* anyway.

When my eyes closed and my teeth sank into flesh, there was only ever one person I saw. *Roman.* It wasn't right or fair, but it wasn't something I had any control over. On any given day, I couldn't decide if I hated the half-sired agent or wanted him. Maybe I just hated that I wanted him.

And…there was that guilt again. Spurring me on to do the stupid thing whenever Vin gave me one of his charming, boyish smiles and asked me to open a vein. I knew he'd offer me his neck after, too, which made refusing him even harder.

Collins and Mandy were really more than enough, but neither of them was comfortable with the fang-to-flesh action. So, they bled into a cup for me. It got the job done, but…something was missing. I couldn't put my finger on it, the aching pinch of rejection I felt in the pit of my stomach. I didn't experience it with Vin, but my guilt was so thick, how could I feel anything else?

"I don't have to work tomorrow," Vin said as he stood from the dining room table. He crossed the kitchen and stashed the lunch bag of my blood in the refrigerator.

I glanced down at my watch. "Sunrise is in an hour."

"Right." He blinked stiffly.

A human girlfriend could have lain in bed with him all day, or gone for a walk in the park, or done any number of normal couple things. I, on the other hand, would be dead until the sun set. Dead and *alone*. The thought of Vin snuggling my cold, unconscious body freaked me right the hell out.

I sucked in my bottom lip and watched him from across the kitchen, waiting patiently. This was the part where he was supposed to offer me his blood, and I was yearning for it. Either because he'd taken so much of mine, or because I knew this would likely be the last time I snacked on him. At least for three months. Maybe forever.

Vin slipped his glasses off and set them on the counter. Then he undid the top few buttons of his polo, his lips twitching up into a suggestive grin. A different brand of hunger than my own lit his eyes. He was just as eager to give his blood as I was to take it.

Even if this couldn't work out, I would miss Vin. The familiarity. The easy comfort food. The genuine care he took to make sure I survived this strange nightmare that was my new reality.

I pushed my guilt and gratitude aside and stood to follow him back to my bedroom, ready to sate my thirst before sending him off and dying with the dawn.

Chapter Two

Road trips at night sucked. The highway was lined with semis and reckless asshats who had clearly been on the road for too long. Or who were *drunk*, I decided as we passed a weaving car that was halfway on the shoulder. Their turn signal had been flashing for five miles.

Collins whipped his blue Toyota RAV4 around a questionable pickup truck with a burnt-out taillight, shooting the driver a stern look as we breezed past in the right lane. Mandy leaned across his lap and pressed her middle finger up against the driver's side window.

"Come on now," Collins said, nudging her out of his personal space.

Mandy huffed and flopped back in her seat, her mousy ponytail poking through the gap under the headrest. She stuck her opposite hand out her own window, twining her fingers through the air rather than giving the shitty drivers a piece of her mind. Her fingertips were stained orange from the bag of Cheetos she'd inhaled in the first half hour of our trip.

"Sure is beautiful country," Collins said for the fifth time, good-humored sarcasm seeping through his words. He winked at me in the rearview mirror.

I rolled my eyes and pushed my earbuds in deeper before pressing play on my phone.

"¿Quién es tu creador?" a feminine, Spanish voice asked.

"Who is your sire?" a masculine, English voice echoed.

I hit repeat and mouthed the words to myself as a headache formed along the base of my skull. I hadn't expected to find Spanish lessons on the chip Roman had given me, but it made sense. That didn't mean I was happy about it.

There were only a few other files on the disk in addition to the crash language course—including several paintings and photographs of dear ol' Pablo and his home back in Spain. I also found dated sets of notes regarding the training regimen at the bat cave.

It took a little reading before I understood why Roman would care how the course had evolved since he passed it fifty years prior. Once he was turned, he would have to pass it again as a vampire. Bummer.

Mandy twisted around in her seat and lifted both eyebrows at me as she shoved a Dorito into her mouth. "Find anything about wolfy training in there?" she shouted to be heard.

I sighed and paused the Spanish lesson before popping out my earbuds. "Just that the program is called Canine Aptitude Training." I shrugged.

Mandy gave me a level glare. "Canine Aptitude Training? Abbreviated C-A-T? You can't be serious."

Collins snickered, and Mandy's evil eye shifted to him.

"And what about this clown's program? Did they get clever while naming that one, too?"

"No idea. I don't see a name, though it seems pretty similar to the vamp program, as far as I can tell," I said, scrolling through the files on my phone for another look. "It's just a watered-down, mortal version. Roman passed it fifty years ago, but the notes he's been keeping since are all about the vamp training."

"That was really cool of him to share," Collins said, stealing another glance in the rearview mirror. His keen, green eyes had been watching me off-and-on throughout the trip.

I pressed my lips together and nodded. "Yeah." I didn't voice out loud what I really thought of Roman's help. How I was pretty sure he was just covering his own ass so I didn't bring him down with me if my true lineage were discovered.

Mandy's brow pinched, and she gave me a warning frown. We hadn't shared the full truth with the newest member of my blood harem. Collins didn't know that my sire was the exiled Baron of House Lilith. Or that Mandy had killed him—and *eaten* him—right after he murdered me. Her revenge snack had been messy enough to result in the freak accident of my transformation, and now…here we were.

The Toyota slowed as we passed through Columbia, and Mandy's expression softened. She gazed out at the shopping mall where Serena worked part-time. She wouldn't be there tonight. My late partner's daughter spent her weekends in St. Louis, visiting her mother and Mandy.

I still wasn't sure how I felt about the girls' blossoming romance. About keeping another bombshell secret from the Banks family. Serena couldn't know that her father had been murdered by a vampire. She couldn't know that I *was* a vampire, or that she was dating a werewolf. If one secret came to light, the others would soon follow. I was sure of it. And I couldn't bear it.

Serena had experienced enough life changes and heartache lately. We all had.

I'd never been through Kansas. I'd never been much of anywhere, really. But everyone I knew who had crossed the Sunflower State complained of the flat, boring view. Farmland that stretched like an endless sea of nothing in all directions.

I couldn't tell for certain—not in the darkness that coated everything beyond the highway. I considered attempting to activate my blood vision, but I didn't want to waste the gift or the energy on something so trivial.

The waning, gibbous moon rose behind us slowly, painting blue shadows over the nothingness I strained to see. It'd been full just a few nights ago when Mandy had shifted and chased the neighbor's cat through the backyard. I didn't have the heart to ask if she'd caught it.

A cluster of city lights brightened our trip here and there, and then the blinking beacons atop a span of commercial windmills snagged my attention. They looked alien and mysterious—like a warning of what lay ahead.

I spent the remainder of the drive attempting to learn Spanish—the slapdash Dracula version, anyway.

"Soy un vampiro."

"I am a vampire."

"Necesito sangre."

"I need blood."

"¿A qué hora es el amanecer?"

"What time is sunrise?"

By the time we took the exit for Salina, I was ready to chuck my phone out the window. I'd barely passed English in school. There was no way I would master Spanish well enough to convince anyone that Pablo had deemed me scion material.

We passed an IHOP and a few hotels, and soon, blue-tinged darkness swallowed us again. Collins turned the Toyota down a gravel road. We passed a mailbox with no numbers and continued on for several miles without seeing so much as a driveway.

"You're sure Roman gave you the right directions?"

Collins asked, glancing at me in the rearview mirror. "We don't have to leave Kansas, do we, Toto?"

Mandy turned around in her seat and pinched her nose. Her eyes watered as she rasped her next breath. "Roadkill. That's definitely skunk."

"That's what you get for leaving your window down." I smirked and crinkled my own nose as the smell reached me, drifting in along with gravel dust. Collins gave Mandy a pointed look.

"Well, I can't roll it up now," she balked. "The smell will be trapped in here with us."

"What's that?" I pressed my face up against my window, taking in the outline of a farmhouse as it came into view. It was a two-story with a wide front porch. Yellow light spilled from every window. As the Toyota rolled closer, I heard faint piano music playing. "This is it."

"How can you be so sure?" Collins' brow creased as he gave the farmhouse a skeptical frown.

"It's three in the morning, and the place is lit up like the Fourth of July," I said. "You do the math."

Mandy gave him a grave nod. "I can smell it—another vampire, not more roadkill," she clarified. She sniffed deeper. "A few humans, too."

Another mailbox marked the driveway leading up to the farmhouse, and this one was painted with two curly, blue Cs.

As we turned off, musical laughter joined the piano, filtering through a screen door on the side of the house. The stoop was covered by a tiny awning, and from it hung a sign that matched the lettering on the mailbox.

The Cottage Crypt was spelled out this time, though the sign was poorly lit and hardly visible from the road. There hadn't been a listing for it online, and there was nothing but farmland for miles around. If someone weren't actively looking for this place, they'd never find it.

Collins followed the driveway back to a small parking area in front of a detached garage. A vintage, slightly rusty Chevy Bel Air and a nicer—yet equally vintage—Rolls Royce took up most of the space, leaving just enough room for the Toyota. Gravel faded into weeds beyond the glow of a security light fixed to the peak of the garage roof.

I waited for Collins to kill the engine and then climbed out to stretch my legs and take another look around. A clothesline draped with sheets and towels cut through the backyard, but before that was a small garden and sitting area. It was lit up like the house, displaying an arched bench trellis with night-blooming flowers and a bubbling fountain.

"Cozy," Mandy said, taking in the very normal scene with me while Collins locked up the car.

"Let's make sure they have room for us before we unpack our luggage," he said, fingering his hair and smoothing the seatbelt creases in his shirt. The snug material hugged his chest, showing off the faint lines of his muscled pecs.

The piano music stopped, and hushed voices trickled out to us as we climbed the few steps under the sign. Through the screen door, I noticed a faded sofa set against busy, floral wallpaper. A lamp on a side table illuminated a stack of magazines and a rotary telephone on the wall.

Before I could press the button for the doorbell, the screen door flew open, and an ancient, shriveled woman peered up at me. Her white hair was coiled in a bun so tight that it stretched her papery skin back in an alarming facelift, made all the more eerie by her eager grin and wide, glossy eyes.

"Welcome," she squealed. Her voice was high-pitched, and I was almost surprised when she didn't follow up her greeting with a wicked-witch cackle. "You must be the crowd Roman called about. Jenny, is it?"

"Jenna." I frowned as I took her outstretched hand. It felt like a cold bundle of sticks, the knuckles knobby and fingers stiff, but there was strength in her shake. "These are my— friends. Max and Mandy."

Mandy stood stock-still beside me, nostrils flaring. *Vampire.* Without my blood vision, I couldn't see it. But Mandy's nose didn't lie. Collins seemed to pick up on it, too, though he offered up a timid smile, ever the gentleman. The old lady winked at him before her eyes darted back to me.

"No need to be shy around here, Jen. We know what's what," she said. "I'm Delilah. Why don't you come on in and meet my *friends*." She hobbled back a few steps and held the screen door open, beckoning us inside.

The stuffy sitting room opened into a larger space with hardwood floors and a gaudy, crystal chandelier. Several small tables were pushed up against one wall. A fainting couch and an upright piano filled the opposite side of the room. There was more busy wallpaper in here, but the swirly gold design was less offensive than the floral menagerie we'd just passed through.

A woman in a sequined flapper dress appeared as we entered the room. She looked like a younger version of Lydia, the woman I'd drank from at the vampire club, Bleeders. My heart raced at the memory, and I silently reminded myself that I'd already eaten tonight—half a cup of Collins' lukewarm A-positive before we embarked on our trip.

"Cal's making up a fresh bed now, Dee," the woman said.

Delilah nodded, but I cut her off before she could introduce the newcomer.

"We're going to need three beds, actually." I blushed.

"Very well." She waved a hand at the other woman. "Go help Cal set up the other two rooms, Stella."

The flapper hurried off, her heels clacking on the staircase that stretched upward behind the fainting couch and piano. I watched her go—maybe a little too intently—until Delilah cleared her throat.

"I share my harem, but it costs extra." She smirked and straightened her navy cardigan. "Angus serves breakfast at four. Richens the blood for a little nightcap before we *nocturnals* retire for the day," she added, taking note of Collins' raised eyebrow. An amused glint slipped into her expression, as if she had suddenly realized just how green we were.

"Wonderful," Collins said, clapping his hands together. "I'll just go grab our luggage then?" He shot me a questioning look, and I nodded my approval.

"I'll help." Mandy turned on her heel and followed him back through the sitting room, leaving me alone with Delilah.

The old vampire clucked her tongue as she watched them go. She gave me a pitying smile. "I struggled with the intimacy at first, too, dear. My generation was especially squeamish about such *relations*. But, if this old bat can learn to fly, so can you." She patted my shoulder, ignoring my flaming face, and turned toward an arched entrance at the back of the foyer. "I'll go let Angus know he'll have two extra mouths to feed. Stella will be down in a moment to show you to your rooms."

I managed to croak out a weak, "Thank you," before she slipped out of sight. The sudden silence sent my insecurities echoing through my head.

Was intimacy really so necessary when it came to feeding?

Was I missing out on some vital part of being a proper vampire? The transition from bagged blood to freshly drawn had been a monumental leap for me as it was.

I only fed fang-to-flesh from Vin, and even that had been difficult at first, but I'd grown comfortable with it over the past few weeks. We were dating, so the intimacy didn't seem like such an awkward notion. How the hell was that supposed to work with an entire harem? Especially with a harem that had no interest in being intimate with me either?

My thoughts drifted to Roman, pausing on the memory of his silky blood as it coated my tongue. My head cradled in the bend of his arm, shoulder blades pressed to the tops of his thighs. I shivered and hugged myself.

Stella returned to the foyer at the same time Collins and Mandy dragged our luggage in from the car. Collins carried my duffel bag over one arm and tugged his large suitcase on wheels behind him. An overstuffed backpack lay against Mandy's shoulders, and tote bags dangled from both of her elbows, one full of garage-sale paperbacks and magazines, the other full of junk food.

"This way," Stella said, opening a pale, slender arm toward the staircase.

I followed first, breathing in the fruity, cotton candy-scented perfume that trailed behind her. Her hips swayed as she climbed the stairs, sashaying the fringe running along the hem of her sparkly dress. Red pulsed at the edges of my sight, sending a stabbing thrill of panic through my chest. I began to wonder just how much extra Delilah charged for sharing her favorite snacks.

"All of our rooms are outfitted with interior, day-sealing shutters," Stella said as we entered the upstairs hallway. "The two on the left, the starling suite and the raven suite, share a bath, and the one on the right, the owl suite, has its own en suite with a clawfoot tub. The household sleeps in alternating shifts, so someone is always available should a member of your harem need anything at all."

Mandy made a soft snort behind me. She didn't care for the word *harem*. I didn't blame her. Being an unwilling sex slave in a vampire brothel was enough to make one uptight about terminology.

Stella turned to me and folded her hands together under her breasts. She had lovely, bright eyes. Liquid and soft, like Judy Garland's. "Do you have any questions?"

I sucked on my bottom lip for a moment. "Two Blood Vice agents, Roman and Vanessa, stayed here a few months ago. Do you remember them?"

She blinked stiffly as if she had expected a question about fresh towels or pillow mints. "Yes, of course I remember them. Delilah's daughter and her pledged scion have stayed here many times."

Daughter? My mind reeled with the new information, but Stella went on before I could fully process it.

"They always stay in the owl suite. Is there anything…else I can do for you?" she asked, her tone slightly more suggestive. Collins made a noise this time.

"I think we're good. Thank you," I said, dismissing her.

She bowed her head politely and slipped past us, her perfume filling my lungs once more as she sauntered back toward the mouth of the stairs. Again, I thought of Lydia and the cozy, dark booth at Bleeders where she's opened her wrist for me.

"Breakfast is in an hour," Stella said over her shoulder. "Your harem is welcome to join us for the meal." The invitation was directed at me. All conversation at the Cottage Crypt had been so far, I realized. Mandy and Collins were being treated as if they were my underlings, here only to do my bidding.

Collins waited until we were alone in the hallway before dropping my bag to the floor. "What a tart." He put his hands on his hips and sniffed.

"Is there anything…else I can do for you?" Mandy mimicked in an exaggerated, sultry voice. Her skew-neck tee shirt left one shoulder bare, and she rolled it in a mocking flirt.

Even though I knew their jabs weren't meant for me, I felt humiliation sour my stomach. Was it really so awful for someone to crave the same exchange I longed for? My face must have given me away because they both stared at me, surprise widening their eyes with the beginnings of remorse. Before either of them could say another word, I snatched up my bag from where Collins had dropped it.

"I'll take the owl suite," I said, opening the bedroom door. "We'll catch up at sunset. Enjoy breakfast."

I stepped inside and closed the door, letting the darkness cloak me until I heard Mandy and Collins shuffle into the opposite rooms. Once my calm returned, I clicked on the bedroom light and took a look around. Only then did Stella's words settle in my mind.

They always stay in the owl suite.

Roman and Vanessa had shared this room. Last spring. My eyes roved over the tarnished brass bedframe, the denim quilt laid across the mattress, the faded wallpaper printed with blue and gray feathers, the antique vanity in the corner.

He'd said Vanessa wasn't his girlfriend, but perhaps she had been, not so terribly long ago. Maybe he'd been reluctant to recommend the bed and breakfast for that very reason. Maybe this room—this entire place—was a big mistake.

My heart trembled pathetically. I had no right to feel betrayed by Roman, yet I was wounded just the same. And I couldn't seem to move from my spot in front of the bedroom door. I couldn't bring myself to invade the space and stir up whatever memories might be lying in wait. I wondered if it was too late to trade rooms with Mandy or Collins.

As if summoned by the thought, I heard their doors creak open. Soft footsteps paused outside my room, and Collins loosed a heavy sigh.

"She's probably checking in with Vin," Mandy whispered. "She can't have the food anyway. Why would she want to watch us eat?"

"Yeah, you're probably right," Collins whispered back.

Their footsteps resumed, fading as they headed downstairs to eat with Delilah's harem.

Tears stung in the corners of my eyes. I was too proud—or maybe too ashamed—to face them just yet. Which meant I was trapped in this room. At least until sunrise. Maybe the awkwardness would die at dawn when I did. I could hope.

I should call Vin, I thought. Maybe it would shake me out of the downward spiral I was stuck in.

I dropped my duffel bag on the denim bedspread and took a slow breath. This was just a room. Just an ordinary room. Lots of people had probably slept here.

My holster grated my hip as I unhooked it from the waistband of my jean shorts and deposited it on the night table. I dug my cell phone out of my back pocket next before sitting on the edge of the bed and pulling my legs up to cross them. Then I uncrossed them and put my feet back on the floor.

My restlessness only seemed to grow as I dialed Vin's number.

"How's the vampire hotel?" he asked by way of greeting.

"It's a B&B," I reminded him. "And it's fine. I guess."

"Do you miss me yet?" he asked next, his voice dropping to a sensual whisper.

"Of course I do." My heart ached at the lie, fueling the fires of shame that were steadily burning through my chest cavity. "I thought you had to work tonight. I was expecting your voicemail to pick up."

"I called in," he said breathlessly, and I realized his whispering wasn't completely to do with seducing me. "I think I made a breakthrough tonight in the lab, I—"

"You"—I snapped, cutting him off before he said something damning—"should probably share this with me when I get back. It sounds like a surprise best revealed *in person.*"

"Oh? Oh! Yes, of course." He cleared his throat and swallowed loud enough for me to hear through the phone. "I can't wait. It's so exciting. Gosh, three months. The anticipation—"

"Will make it even better," I assured him, hoping like hell my suspicions were wrong and we weren't being listened to by whoever the vampire equivalent of the NSA was. That seemed like a pretty fast way to end my new career before it even began. My paranoia felt extra justified when I recalled

Roman's extensive FBI resources as a Blood Vice agent.

A soft knock had me nearly jumping out of my skin, and panic hiked that paranoia into overdrive. But when Stella's muffled voice crooned through the door, some other emotion took hold of me.

"What was that?" Vin asked.

"Uh, housekeeping," I answered under my breath as I slid off the bed. "I asked for fresh towels. I'm going to take a shower before heading to bed."

"We'll talk more tomorrow?"

"Yeah, yeah. Have a good day," I said.

"Sweet dreams," he said, the farewell clipping off suddenly as I ended the call.

"Ms. Skye?" Stella called as she knocked again. I cracked the door open.

"Y-yes?" My mouth was painfully dry. I licked my lips and tried to smile at her.

"Dee wanted to offer you a drink—on the house." Her voice was sweeter than before, as if she wanted to be sure I understood that she was offering herself to me as a kind gesture. *A pity drink,* I scoffed to myself. And just when I thought I couldn't sink any lower.

Ragtime piano music bubbled up from downstairs. It was loud and playful.

"Your harem is enjoying a little entertainment," Stella

explained, that alluring edge seeping into her gaze. Their entertainment was our privacy.

A shiver rocked my shoulders, but she acted as though she hadn't noticed. She was using kid gloves. *Vampling* gloves. But I *was* a vampling. Maybe letting a veteran donor treat me like one wasn't such a bad thing. After all, I hadn't minded so much when Lydia had done it.

I opened the door wider and invited Stella inside.

Chapter Three

Lydia was no veteran donor, I decided after letting Stella into my room. The flapper presented her wrist to me like a bottle of champagne, holding a white cloth beneath it with her opposite hand. We sat side-by-side on the edge of the bed, her sequined dress pressed against my jean shorts and bare knee. Nothing but the distant piano music to keep the silence at bay.

"I don't often feed from strangers. Or straight from the vein," I said. The confessions didn't faze her.

"I gathered as much from your harem's behavior."

"Sorry." I gave her a sheepish smile.

"They are young. So are you. Give it time," she said, shifting beside me. My head swam with the scent of her perfume. This close, I was keenly aware of the depth in her gaze. Was she half-sired like Roman? I had to know.

"How old are you?" I asked before I could think better of it.

Stella's laughter rippled across my skin. "My, my. You are *quite* young, aren't you? I didn't think that was considered a polite question even by human standards."

"Sorry." I glanced down at my lap while my brain searched for something less nosy to ask her, but a million invasive questions begged for answers. As an officer, I'd been expected to ask prying questions. It'd been my job. I was no good at beating around bushes.

"I'm one hundred and twenty-three." Stella lowered her arm, resting it across my legs with a relenting sigh. "Dee ran a speakeasy during prohibition. Cal, Angus, and I were in her employ. She'd lost her only child—or so she'd thought—during the Civil War. So we became her children. She took good care of us misfits." Stella chuckled but then fell solemn. "When Dee grew ill, there was nothing we could do. That's when Vanessa returned—"

"Wait, Vanessa was her *human* daughter? Delilah didn't sire her?"

Stella shook her head. "*Au contraire*, Vanessa sired Delilah." She hiccupped a soft laugh. "Mother and child are now scion and sire."

"What a strange world we live in."

"It gets stranger every day," Stella said, nodding in agreement. "Dee's speakeasy was raided in her absence, and we were thrown in jail. By the time we got out, Vanessa had Dee set up here." She waved her hand around the room. "We didn't have anywhere else to go, and when Dee revealed what had happened to her and what she was in need of—well, I won't say it was a natural transition. But we got through it." She smiled fondly at the memories of the past.

"And…the intimacy?" I couldn't resist prying further. Like she hadn't shared enough already. "How long did that take to get through?"

Stella blinked at me, and her lips curled in amused understanding. "There are all kinds of intimacy. The variety shared between lovers is a far cry from that shared between mother and child, or friends for that matter."

My face flushed, the heat spreading down into my chest until I felt sweat prickle along my collarbone. Stella's hand in my lap turned and gripped my knee.

"Don't be embarrassed," she said gently. "You're familiar with Freud's Oedipus complex?" I nodded, my voice frozen by humiliation. "It's very similar. It affects new vampires *and* new donors."

"I—we don't know how to get around it," I said, unable to meet her gaze.

Stella sighed and moved her hand from my knee to my arm, massaging her fingers into my shoulder. "Do you enjoy back rubs?" she asked.

"I-I guess?"

"When you go to a massage parlor, do you feel sexually aroused by the person massaging you?"

I shook my head.

"And when you were human and ate a meal at your favorite restaurant, did you feel compelled to sleep with the chef?" she asked.

"That's different."

"Is it? Does it not make you feel good? Relaxed? Satisfied?"

"Well, yeah, but…" I met her knowing gaze and huffed. "Do you not feel…aroused when someone drinks from you?"

She tilted her head from side to side. "Sometimes. Depends on the vampire." Her grin grew mischievous. Lydia had made me feel something I never thought I would for a woman. But when I really dissected my attraction to her, it was her blood more than anything else that I craved.

"I'm not really into women that way," I said.

She raised an eyebrow. "I didn't offer myself to you *that way.*"

My cheeks warmed, and my stomach fluttered as I tried to relax. Stella extended her wrist in front of me again, and I took her arm in my hands this time, holding the linen around it like a wrapper around a burger. Thinking of her in this way took some of the tension out of the act, but it also made it feel more degrading.

I lowered my mouth but paused to look up at her for some final notion of consent. She dipped her chin in a soft nod. It was all I needed. My fangs popped free, and I sank them into the shallow meat of her wrist.

Blood welled instantly, like juice rising up from a ripe plum. Stella remained perfectly still. Her breath and pulse were steady. Slow even. She'd been doing this for over a hundred years, and it showed in more than her disciplined calm.

Her blood was rich. Like Roman's. Maybe even richer. She was older than he was, after all. But where Roman's blood had been fed to me in an act of desperation and survival, Stella's was unnecessary and offered with quiet patience.

And unlike Vin, she expected nothing from me in return. Not sex. Not money. Not a vial of my own blood.

I wondered if I would ever be comfortable enough with Mandy and Collins to share a moment like this with either of them. Maybe I'd formed my harem too suddenly, out of need rather than waiting for people with the right…rapport. Some friends made bad lovers, and vice versa. Maybe the same applied to friends and blood donors.

After I'd had my fill of Stella, I slowly pulled my fangs free and wrapped her arm with the linen. The blood soaked through the material, but it didn't spread far. And after a second, she swiped it across her skin, cleaning the remaining blood and revealing two pink circles of flesh. I blinked, and the marks were gone.

She grinned and winked at my surprise. "Perks of the job."

"I can smell her on you." Mandy folded her arms in the front passenger seat of the Toyota and refused to look at me as we pulled out of the Cottage Crypt's driveway.

By the time I'd risen, the two of them had already supped with Delilah's harem. Cal, the dashing piano player, had offered to take my duffel bag out to the car, but Collins collected it before I could answer. He seemed almost as agitated as Mandy.

"I would have given you some blood if you'd asked," she said, the tips of her ears turning pink.

I shrugged. "I thought you'd appreciate the break."

"I'm a werewolf. I don't need a break, and my blood is better than a *human's* anyway."

"Hey, now." Collins sat up straighter in the driver's seat.

"Are you jealous?" I asked, unable to keep the shock out of my voice. "I thought you hated the idea of opening a vein for a bloodsucker?"

"That was before I met you!" Mandy threw her hands in the air and twisted around in her seat. "I *offered* to be part of your harem. Remember?"

"What is the problem here?" I said, feeling oddly defensive. "Do you think I should have asked your permission first or something?"

"No!" Mandy shouted back at me.

"I think what she's trying to say, Skye," Collins said in a

more even if tight voice, "is that we're a team. *You* make us a team. And when you step outside of our circle, it makes us all vulnerable."

A chill gripped my insides. "Did I miss something? Did something happen?"

Mandy snorted and angled around again. "Granny Fangs tried to take a bite out of him after breakfast."

"What?" I shrieked. My blood vision flashed alive in a hot, angry burst. Had Stella been a diversion? Was her free drink a setup so Delilah could get a little strange from my own harem? Was this sickening feeling scouring my insides betrayal…or was I just as jealous as I'd accused Mandy of being?

"She didn't try," Collins quickly amended. "But she hinted that she'd like to, more or less."

"Mmmhmm." Mandy reached over the center console and pinched his cheek. "I could just eat this one right up," she teased in a creaky, old voice.

Collins nudged her away with his shoulder. "I'm driving here, kid." His eyes met mine in the rearview mirror, and he frowned. "Are you all right, Skye? Your eyes look…different."

"I'm fine." My blood vision slowly faded. I could make out the green of his eyes and the soft brown sweep of his hair once more. "I didn't mean to leave you guys out in the open like that," I said, blowing out a slow sigh. "I just... Stella let me drink from her wrist."

Collins cleared his throat. "I get it. And hey, maybe we'll eventually work our way up to that."

"Speak for yourself," Mandy grumbled. "I like you, Jenna, but that's just too much like what I went through before." She glanced over her shoulder, panic tightening her expression. "You understand, right?"

"Of course." I smiled and reached out to squeeze her arm. "It's fine. Really."

"And you've always got Vin," Collins added. "For the times you need a little more *touch* with your meals."

I cringed, remembering how I'd lied to him when Stella had come to my door. He'd been wigged out about Lydia, and that had been for an undercover job. If he knew that I'd fed from Stella for no other reason than I wanted to, he would not be thrilled.

"What's wrong with Vin?" Collins asked, interpreting my silence the way a therapist might.

"I'm breaking up with him when we get back from Denver." Something about saying it out loud made it feel more finite. And more tragic. But at the same time, I felt a weight lift off my shoulders. This had to be done.

"Suckage." Mandy's hand pressed down on top of mine where it lay on her arm. She gave me a pitying frown. "I guess it's a double whammy with him being a blood donor, too, huh?"

I leaned back in my seat and pressed the side of my head to the cool glass of the window. "I'll figure something out. It wouldn't be right to stay with him just for his blood."

"Don't put on the red light just yet, Roxanne," Collins said, eyeballing me in the mirror. "Let's get through this training course first."

Mandy sighed and leaned over to dig through her bag of snacks on the floorboard. She ripped open a bag of pork rinds and clicked on the radio.

The highway was mostly empty. And flat. And straight. With nothing else to do but wallow in self-pity, I dug my phone and earbuds out.

"*¿Dónde está el burdel de sangre más cercano?*" the digital Spanish tutor greeted me.

"Where is the nearest blood brothel?" her English assistant echoed. That's what I wanted to know.

I played it again, committing it to memory should I ever find myself thirsty and alone in Mexico. Then I wondered if Denver had its own version of Bleeders.

Collins and Mandy wouldn't be vulnerable if I didn't take them with me.

Chapter Four

"What the hell kind of airport is this?" I stared out the back window of the Toyota, my neck craning so I could look up at the monstrous, blue horse statue whose laser-red eyes observed the traffic below.

"That's Blucifer," Mandy said around a mouthful of popcorn. She'd snagged the treat along with a tourist guide at the last gas station we'd filled up at. "Says here, the thing is cursed." She slapped the back of her buttery hand to the magazine page. "Even killed the guy who made it."

Collins nodded. "If old blue gives you the heebie-jeebies, you should see the gruesome pieces displayed *inside* the airport."

"We'll have to skip the morbid art tour. Kai's meeting us in the parking garage." A creepy shiver rattled my spine as I gave the demonic statue my back and took in the strange terminal sprawling beyond it. The novel architecture of the roof made it look like a few dozen giant teepees had been crammed together, their white canvases glowing under the looming moon.

According to Roman's notes, the Blood Authority Training Center was nearly impossible to find. The entrance was located off a defunct baggage tunnel from the airport's faulty first run at an automated system. The notes hinted at the possibility of some government bunker hidden beneath the airport, too. But as long as the apocalypse kept its distance, the BATC officials didn't have to worry about sharing the bat cave.

Collins braked as we entered the east parking garage, letting the Toyota crawl past the rows and rows of vehicles. It was pushing four in the morning, so we didn't encounter too many travelers. Just a winding, endless sea of cars, packed in tightly to await their owners' returns from whatever business or pleasure had sent them jetting off across the country.

I counted down the numbers and levels, helping Collins search for our designated spot. We were an hour earlier than the time in the admittance letters requested we arrive. *Make that two hours,* I noted, as the time zone updated on the screen of my cell phone. But when the Toyota was finally parked, and we stepped out to stretch our legs, Kai Natani was waiting. His bald head shone brightly in the harsh overhead lighting.

If I hadn't known he'd be meeting us, I wouldn't have recognized him. The black fatigues he wore were a stark contrast to the fancy suit he'd prowled around in at Nigel's party. Though the cocky confidence was familiar.

"Eager thing, aren't you?" His voice echoed through the garage as he reached out to take my hand. I didn't consider myself dainty by any means, but Kai was a beast. His sausage-sized fingers engulfed mine, and he gave me a jarring shake that I strained to smile through. No flirty knuckle kisses this time.

"We meet again." I cracked a more genuine smile once my hand was back in my possession.

"Mr. Collins and Ms. Starsgard, I take it?" Kai said, reaching out to greet them next. Mandy looked ready to bolt, her chest swelling and eyes dilating. It was the same reaction she always had when encountering a new vampire. But then a hard mask slipped over her features, and her jaw clenched as she let Kai take her hand and give it the perfunctory shake.

"Have many others arrived yet?" I asked, dropping my voice when Kai gave me a pointed look.

"Grab your gear," he said. "I'll fill you in on the ride."

I swallowed and nodded, remembering that we were in a public parking garage, however deserted it might appear.

We grabbed our bags out of the Toyota and silently followed Kai through an unmarked service door. A massive elevator waited on the other side, along with a concrete set of stairs leading up and another going down.

Kai directed us toward the elevator, where he swiped a keycard hanging from his belt down the front of a small, black box on the wall. The elevator opened, and he led us inside. The lift was big enough for at least two-dozen full-grown men.

"One more minute," Kai said at my questioning gaze, as if he suspected we were being listened to. Once we stepped out into the sub-basement level, he marched us around the corner and down a dark passage with poor lighting that flickered every so often. Somewhere nearby, I heard a pipe drip.

The offending smell of mildew and gasoline slowed my pace, and from the corner of my eye, I watched Mandy cover her mouth and nose. Collins squeezed her shoulder with his free hand and then tucked away the handle of his wheeled suitcase before lifting it off the grimy concrete.

Not long after, Kai stopped at the mouth of a tunnel, where…a golf cart waited.

The image seemed to tickle Mandy.

"To the Batmobile," she whispered over my shoulder. I sucked in a tight breath to keep from laughing as Kai gave us an annoyed scowl. I was sure it wasn't the first time someone had made the joke.

The contraption was a larger, luxurious model that I was sure many a celebrity frequented the fairways in, but Kai dwarfed the thing. His hulking shoulders filled most of the front row and extended a few inches outside the driver's side opening.

"Well? All aboard," he said, slapping the seat beside him.

Mandy quickly filed into the backseat, deliberately ignoring the invitation. Collins tried to be less obvious as he circled the cart and took the spot beside her, leaving me to take up the narrow perch next to Kai.

He grinned at me as he twisted the keys in the ignition, and then we were off, whizzing through winding tunnels that seemed to be on a slight decline. I clutched my bag in my lap with one hand and gripped the edge of my seat with the other as we took a sharp turn without slowing. If not for the full-capacity weight to hold it down, I was sure it would have tipped over.

"You're early," Kai said, his voice booming above the high-pitched whine of the engine. "The recruits from House Hanson arrived just before you, but the rest are yet to come. It's a small lot this season. Two wolves, four humans, and six vampires." He shook his head as if disappointed. "They're an unusually young lot, too. I suppose that's why the duke was so willing to include you and your brood, unprepared as you are."

The insult lacked malice, but it stung, knowing we'd been scraped from the bottom of the barrel. I bit the inside of my cheek and kept my mouth shut. Telling Kai off was not the way to gain favor—and I had a feeling I was going to need all the help I could get over the next three months. Roman had said most of the vampire recruits spent fifty years with their sires before being admitted. I had a summer under my belt and a mostly self-taught vampling 101 crash course. Calling me unprepared was being kind.

"As a new vampling, it's no surprise that you still have your human name," Kai went on. "And being orphaned so young, it would be understandable if you eventually pledged yourself to another household. In the meantime, you'll all be addressed as recruits from House Zajalvo."

Collins perked up at the topic of my late sire. I'd given him the shorthand lie Roman had constructed for me. Nothing more. It was safest that way.

"Here we are." Kai slowed the cart as we neared the end of the tunnel. Bright light flooded the exit. I squinted as we emerged from it, taking in the cavernous space.

It was like the inside of an enormous warehouse. Even brightly lit, there were sections of the ceiling that faded into shadows, spanning at least ten stories over our heads. A pathway, wide enough for a pair of golf carts to fit through, wound between dozens of squat buildings. In the far distance, on the opposite side of the training base, the structure appeared unfinished—*no, not unfinished,* I realized after looking closer.

It was the domed mouth of a cave. A huge cave. As if the engineers had dissected it right down the middle, and then decided that it was too beautiful to hollow out for their top-secret facility. Purple and blue-tinged crystals crusted the curved wall. The smooth, flat concrete enclosing the rest of the space tapered off at both sides and the ceiling, bleeding into the natural façade. Through a gap in the buildings, I spied a dark body of water sunk into the floor under the haunting cave ceiling.

"You'll be staying in separate barracks designated for each program," Kai said. He braked as we neared a row of plain, windowless buildings. The doors were unmarked, but I supposed if this place were ever discovered by the muggles— or whatever they called the humans who weren't in the know—it would be marginally easier to explain away if *HERE BE VAMPIRES* wasn't spelled out for them.

A tall, black woman in fatigues and a matching beret saluted Kai as the golf cart rolled to a stop in front of her. "Chief," she greeted him as her dark eyes assessed us.

"Sergeant," Kai said, tossing a casual salute back at her. Then he twisted his massive frame around to look at Mandy. "This is your stop, Starsgard. Sergeant Carmichael oversees our canine training division."

Mandy pressed her lips together and gave me a pleading look.

"Good luck," I whispered and squeezed her hand.

"Starsgard, is it?" Sergeant Carmichael asked as Mandy climbed out of the golf cart. The woman had a bit of an accent. British, perhaps.

"Yes…ma'am?" Mandy squeaked.

"This way." She turned on her booted heels and marched

through the doorway of the nearest building. Mandy hurried to keep up, flinging her knapsack over her shoulder.

We dropped off Collins next, to a pale man in matching black fatigues. He was stacked almost as well as Kai, but with hair as white as Roman's. I wondered if he was half-sired, but I felt it would be too rude to ask him outright.

"The vampire barracks is at the other end of the facility," Kai said. "I'm afraid you won't be seeing much of your harem during training, though there are a few group exercises in the last month."

My back straightened. "I won't be seeing much of them? You mean other than to feed?"

Kai shook his head. "The mortal recruits don't give blood during training."

"Uh…" This was going to pose a problem.

"There's a communal harem," he said, one corner of his mouth hitching up in a teasing grin. "Many of the houses send their own donors, but for a nominal fee, some choose the simplicity of feeding on the resident bleeders."

"Nominal fee?" I winced. My savings were being stretched thin as it was, having to cover the bills for the three months Mandy and I would be gone. We'd canceled the Wi-Fi and cable, and the thermostat was set to kick the furnace on only if the temperature dropped below fifty degrees.

"An anonymous sponsor covered your harem dues," Kai

said. My neck snapped as I jerked my head around to gawk at him.

"Who?"

"And that's why they're called anonymous." He snorted. "You'll have first pick, seeing as how you're so early."

"But House Hanson—"

"Brought their own," Kai injected before nodding his chin at a building we were fast approaching. It was bigger than the others, which made sense. The vampire program was the largest, considering they made up seventy percent of all Blood Vice agents, and I guessed that this communal harem would be included in the layout, as well.

Kai parked the golf cart in a small lot beside the building and killed the engine. I was about to ask if he oversaw the vampire program when he glanced down at his watch.

"Sergeant Sorano should be here soon," he said.

"Vanessa?" My voice broke. Roman's *ex* was going to be my trainer?

"Faye Sorano," Kai amended, narrowing his eyes at me. My poker face needed all kinds of work. "Vanessa's sire," he added, smothering my relief.

"Okay." It wasn't like I could object, and quitting wasn't an option. I shifted my body, trying to get comfortable on the small square of bench seat. "What is it that *you* do here?"

Kai leaned back and folded his arms over his chest. "I'm

a pencil pusher." He barked out a jolting laugh at my surprise.

"But…Sergeant Carmichael called you Chief."

"It's a nickname." His laughter tapered. "I instruct the law course. I also supervise the recruits and records divisions and assist with the program finals."

I didn't know what to say. I wanted to be angry with Roman for misleading me and making me look like a fool…but when I really thought about it, he *had* introduced Kai as an instructor rather than a trainer. Clearly, I was capable of looking like a fool all on my own.

Kai glanced at his watch again. "I suppose I could go ahead and take you to the harem for a light repast. I was about to head that way myself," he said, climbing out of the golf cart.

The vehicle rocked, nearly pitching me off the edge of my seat. I gripped the corner pole holding up the roof and sucked in a tight breath. When the vehicle settled, I quickly exited it, threw my duffel bag over my shoulder, and followed Kai through the barracks' entrance.

The narrow hallways were equally bare, with not so much as an awards placard or bulletin board to break up the monotonous, gray concrete that formed every building I'd seen so far. The doors we passed were steel and lacked windows. A few of them were paired with small, black boxes similar to the one that Kai had used his keycard on for the elevator. And a few rooms lacked doors altogether. Kai nodded and announced them as we passed by.

"Sergeant Sorano's quarters, my quarters, laundry, showers." He pointed a finger at the end of the hall. "The cadet crypt is down that way, and the harem is right here." He sighed, his shoulders shivering as he ran his keycard down the front of the black box next to the door.

As we entered the foyer of the harem, my mood perked instantly. The walls were hung with shimmery curtains looped in artful patterns befitting a theater. Incense fogged the air, and exotic music chimed from some unseen speaker. Voices echoed from two adjacent hallways. Soon after, a swarm of humans appeared.

The variety was overwhelming. Some were doe-eyed and bashful, others brazen and flirty. A man in a three-piece suit gave me a reserved smile before beaming at Kai. It occurred to me that the large vampire might prefer donors who could supply him with more blood than the waifish women I'd fed from.

An alarm broke through the music, blaring out three short bursts before falling silent, and Kai swore under his breath.

"Another recruit is arriving," he explained. "I have to go." He waved a hand at the menagerie of donors. "You're allowed to select four. I'd do that now before the others arrive. Then head to the crypt and get settled in a bunk. Lineup is out front at twenty hundred hours. Be early. Faye comes down hardest on whoever takes last place on the first day."

After that, he was gone, back through the open doorway we'd just entered through.

I turned around slowly, taking in the curious eyes awaiting my decision.

Chapter Five

There were a lot of things I missed about being human. Not having to court my food—and not having my food court me—was near the top of the list. The pork chops I put in my shopping cart hadn't rejoiced, and the ones left in the grocery store cooler hadn't sulked. Ah, the good old days.

The longer I stood there, waiting for one of the harem donors to make the first move, the more inexperienced I could tell I appeared in their eyes. A few slunk off, ducking back down either hallway as if they had no interest in servicing a novice. This was a total disaster.

I finally worked up the required nerve to uproot myself and stalked over to a lanky man towering in the corner.

"I'm Jenna," I said, extending my hand. Before he could accept it, a sharp voice made me jump.

"He's taken."

I turned my head to find a gorgeous woman standing in the threshold. Her deep red hair lay in a smooth sheet down to her waist. The color was even more startling against the backdrop of her black, knit sweater. She propped one shoulder on the doorframe and folded her arms, giving me a vicious grin. I'd expected some competition, but honestly, not so soon.

"I was told I had first pick," I said, refusing to retract my hand, even though the man had inched away from me.

"He's from my personal harem." The woman's smile flat-lined. "If you put your filthy fangs on him, I'll be within rights to rip your throat out. From the looks of you, that won't be much of a challenge."

So, she was House Hanson.

"My mistake," I said, holding up my hand in surrender as I took a step back. "I'm Jenna."

"I'm hungry." She flashed her fangs and hissed at me, then swept through the foyer, snatching her harem boy by the arm.

"Guess we won't be braiding each other's hair anytime soon," I grumbled to myself.

One of the remaining donors heard and stifled a snicker with the back of one hand. Her florescent green, high-top sneakers looked radioactive, and her jean vest was so frayed I was sure it wouldn't survive its next wash. If it had ever been washed. Half of her head was shaved, but the hair on the other side sprouted from her part line in a rainbow of brilliant colors, cascading over her shoulder where it ended in a knot of curls. Everything else she sported was black, from her lipstick to the spandex tights squeezing her twiggy legs.

She gave me a shy wave when my eyes finally focused on her face. "Cool top."

"Thanks." I glanced down and realized I was wearing one

of Vin's old softball shirts from the morgue's weekend warrior team. It had been a comfy choice for the car ride, but in retrospect, maybe not the most tasteful apparel for a vampire. It didn't seem to bother Rainbow Brite's estranged, punk-goth cousin.

"Hi, my name is Natalie, and I'm a bleeder," she said as if we were at an AA meeting. "It's been three days since I last let a vamp suck me off."

"Ugh," another of the donors wailed at her, a man with a scruffy goatee. "You're disgusting." He walked off, and I realized it was just Natalie and I left in the foyer, surrounded by the sparkly curtains and awkward silence.

"I like you," she finally said. "Wanna bite me?"

"Why?" I wondered if this were going to be more of a Lydia or Stella situation.

Natalie blinked, considering my question with a thoughtful frown. "It pays well and hurts less than getting a tattoo, but it makes me feel just as macho."

It was an honest enough answer, I guessed. Plus, if I had to pick out four donors, rejecting the only willing one wouldn't be a very good start.

"Yes. I think I'd like to bite you," I said.

Natalie waved her arm, gesturing for me to follow her down the hallway opposite the one that House Hanson's prima donna had taken. Once we were closed away in her small room, I decided to take further advantage of her honesty and set some ground rules.

"I don't sleep with my donors. Is that going to be a problem for you?"

She shrugged one shoulder. "I don't do this for the sex. I told you, it's good money."

I nodded. "Okay. Now I just have to find three more like you who don't suck. Any suggestions?"

"You said suck." She snorted and flopped down on her unmade bed. A crooked Cure poster hung above her headboard, brought to life by the glow of two black light sconces fastened to the wall on either side of it. On her bedside table, a CD player crooned *Gold Dust Woman* next to a doll with bleeding eyes that stood erect inside a coffin-shaped box. Natalie caught me staring and grinned. "Sampson would be another good pick. And maybe Cara and Ned. They're all easygoing and don't care if they get sexed up or not."

"Good. Thanks." I breathed out a shuddering sigh, marveling at the oddness of it all. Would I ever get used to this strange diet? Or was I doomed to be forever awkward, like a pre-pubescent boy shuffling his feet on the sidelines of the dance floor?

"I'll introduce you to them after you do your thing," Natalie said, snatching up a wet wipe from a box beside the creepy doll. She scrubbed her wrist and forearm. "Have you brushed your teeth recently?" she asked.

"Umm, last night when I rose…"

"There's a new brush behind the mirror." She nodded at a pedestal sink in the corner. "Would you mind?"

"No, of course not." I guessed I wasn't the only one with ground rules. But brushing my teeth was far less demanding than sex. I dropped my duffel bag beside her night table and stepped over a Ouija board laid out on the floor on my way to the sink.

"So, how long have you been working at the bat cave?" I asked as I scanned the medicine cabinet for the toothbrush she'd offered.

"A little over two years now." Natalie twirled a finger around one of her rainbow curls. "I'm just doing this to save up for college. My dad drank and gambled his way through the only savings I had to my name as a minor, but he can't touch my BATC paychecks. This time next year, I'll be a full-time student."

"What do you plan to major in?" I asked before loading the toothbrush with paste and stuffing it into my mouth. I smelled the citrus-mint flavor, but I couldn't taste anything. My palate had fully assimilated, and now, the only thing that had any flavor on my tongue was blood.

"Human law—well…" She made a comical face. "I guess it's just considered *law* up top."

"Nice."

She made a different face at my lie. "The only people who think law sounds *nice* are the weirdos who want to pursue it as badly as I do."

I spat into the sink and rinsed my mouth. "Okay, you got me. I was bored to tears in every law class I've ever taken—and I was a police officer."

"Really?" She scooted to the edge of the bed and clapped her hands. "Jackpot! Boy, do I have some questions for you."

"Can they wait until tomorrow?" I asked, giving her an apologetic smile. "I've been on the road for two days."

"Oh, yeah, totally." She straightened as I sat down on the bed beside her.

The arm she offered had looked smooth and unmarred at a distance, but up close, I noticed the odd texture of her skin. Light pink puncture scars riddled her flesh, so pale that in the right lighting, they could have easily gone unnoticed.

"They have the fancy ointments here," Natalie answered before I could ask. "The scar tissue heals up soft, too. So you shouldn't feel any wonky resistance when you bite down."

I'd dealt with my fair share of suicide victims as a cop, and more than one of them had been into self-harm leading up to their deaths. The scars on Natalie's arm put a bad taste in my mouth—figuratively speaking. They reminded me of the wrist-to-elbow, raised column of lines I'd witnessed on the arm of a boy who had hung himself in his aunt's garage. They also reminded me that a similar stack of scars was making its way up Collins' arm.

"Don't you worry about how this…looks?" I frowned at Natalie. She shrugged.

"I'm going to get a tattoo cover-up when I leave here. It will probably hurt more than all the bites put together."

"Who hands out the fancy ointment?" I asked next. Collins would need that soon if he wanted to keep Lazlo from freaking out.

"Marco. Stuffy dude in the suit," she added. "He's the harem supervisor—we all call him Mr. Blueblood. If you ask him, he'll prattle on and on about his royal fourth cousin, thrice-removed. Marco's the only half-sired among us."

I shook my head, trying to make sense of the new information, filtering out the fluff and committing the vital to memory. *Mr. Blueblood, harem supervisor, fancy scar ointment.*

"So…should we give this a whirl, you and I?" Natalie held up her arm again.

I pressed my tongue to the roof of my mouth, tucking it out of the way before extending my fangs. The conversation with Mandy and Collins in the car came back to me, and I hesitated, wondering if I should talk to them about this first. It seemed so…silly. They'd acted as if we were all high school sweethearts, and they were vexed that I'd ditched them for someone who let me get to second base.

"Any time now." Natalie gave me a sweet smile. Her gentle encouragement anchored my common sense.

Collins and Mandy couldn't donate blood during training. This was my only option, and I needed to get over my first sip jitters now. Unless I wanted the entire harem to laugh me out of here.

I bit down without warning, drawing a soft gasp from Natalie. Remorse slugged me, but I waited until I'd finished drinking from her before offering up an apology.

"I'll do better next time," I said, wiping my chin with the back of my hand.

Natalie blushed. "It's all good. I've totally had worse." She grabbed another wet wipe and dabbed at the two new marks on her wrist.

"Really, I know how to be gentle. I was just…nervous."

She smirked at me and reached for a tube of ointment on her night table. "For not sexing me up, you sure talk like you just did."

I grimaced, and my shoulders slouched forward. "I'm terrible at this."

"You're not," she assured me, nudging my shoulder with hers. "Come on. Let's go meet the others before another vamp gets to them first."

The three donors Natalie had recommended seemed nice enough. Sampson, the guy with the scruffy goatee, seemed to equally love and hate her, much like an annoying little sister. Ned and Cara were harder to read, but they accepted my acquisition of them without balking. After Natalie had introduced everyone and we all established that this arrangement would work for the three months I would be there, I headed off to the crypt as Kai had instructed.

There was a black box on the wall beside this metal door, too. I panicked at first, realizing Kai hadn't given me a keycard for access. But as I neared the device, a light flickered green, sensing my motion, and the door unlocked.

An overhead light clicked on, illuminating the room. I'd never seen so much concrete. It devoured everything—walls, floor, ceiling. It had even been used to frame out the few furnishings in the room. There were ten beds, five on either side, composed of thin, white mattresses laid on top of concrete platforms. They were coverless and narrow, their heads butting up against the walls and feet extending out to create a center aisle. No sheets or pillows either. Not that a vampire needed such things in the dead of their unnatural sleep.

Concrete shelves were sandwiched between the bunks. Beneath each one sat a small, digital safe box like those found in many hotels. The hinged doors were open, all except for one in a back corner of the room. I assumed that bed had been claimed by the feisty redhead. Which made my selection of a bunk near the door an easy one.

I dropped my duffel bag onto the mattress and sat down beside it, but my muscles refused to relax. The place made Natalie's gothic lair seem downright cheerful. I breathed in the damp basement stench permeating the air. *Three months.* The grim thought launched a countdown in my mind.

Twelve weeks. I could do this.

I busied myself with unpacking my bag and tucking away anything I deemed valuable into the safe—my sidearm, cell phone, wallet. There was zero reception this far underground, and Roman's notes stated that his most recent contacts had been given limited communication access anyway. And I was pretty sure the only firearms I'd need were the ones the base issued for me to train with. Everything else stayed in my bag that I set on top of the small shelf beside my bed.

My wristwatch buzzed, warning me that sunrise was an hour off. It would alert me again at a quarter till. I considered checking out the showers, but Kai had said to settle into a bunk. So I lay back on the uncomfortable mattress and men-tally sorted through the new Spanish I'd learned on the second leg of the trip here.

It wasn't long before the crypt door hissed open again. I

was relieved to see a new face that didn't belong to evil Red Biting Hood. But like the other small mercies of the night, my relief was premature. The newcomer, a woman with a severe bob of shiny, black hair, hardly spared me half a glance before making her way to a bunk on the opposite wall and three down from mine.

I remembered Roman's advice and bit my tongue, refraining from introducing myself. *Don't try to make friends.*

A few minutes later, another recruit arrived—a tall, black man with a lean, gymnast's build and sharp cheekbones. His eyes regarded me a moment longer than the woman's had, but he only offered a cursory nod before taking the bunk across from mine.

The next time the door opened, I wasn't so lucky.

"I hear some idiot got first pick and settled for all the garbage donors," a hateful, masculine voice crooned.

My breath tightened in my lungs as a square-jawed man entered the crypt alongside the woman from House Hanson. Her cold eyes landed on me.

"Probably the same idiot who tried to claim a member of my personal harem."

The man shook his head and ran a hand through his short, black hair. "We should have waited for spring. Wiping the floor with the competition just isn't as much fun when they're invalids."

His eyes followed the woman's line of sight and paused on me. The smug grin stretching his face widened as the two of them passed my bunk and retreated to the back of the room. He took the bed opposite the one the woman from House Hanson had claimed, leaving three empty bunks between us. Their camaraderie made me wonder if the man was from the same house. Kai had said *recruits*, plural. But since I'd brought a human and a wolf with me, I hated to assume. And I definitely wasn't about to ask.

I put my hands behind my head and stared up at the ceiling, willing the sun to hurry along. Tomorrow would be a new night. I just needed it to get here, that was all. I closed my eyes and silently began mouthing my Spanish lessons again.

"I don't know, Mic," I heard Red whisper to her sidekick. "That bunk near the door looks extra soft. What do you think?"

"You know, Blair, I think you might be right."

Mic and Blair. I filed the names away for future reference. Mic seemed like as much a piece of work as Blair, and I didn't realize he was standing over me until I felt his foot kick the edge of my mattress. He'd moved so fast. It was a struggle not to flinch in surprise.

"Move your shit. I want this bunk."

My blood vision cast a red halo around his face as I opened my eyes to glare up at him. "Then you should have gotten here sooner."

"Seriously. You need to move," he said. A muscle in his neck twitched, and dimples formed on either side of his mouth, though the smile didn't reach his eyes. The other recruits in the room grew still, sensing the tension as it swelled.

"Seriously," I echoed him. "That's not going to happen."

"You think we don't know who you are?" he snapped. "Zajalvo's orphaned vampling has no business training with seasoned scions like us." He kicked the mattress again. "Move."

"Vampling? You're one to speak." The final vampire recruit entered the crypt. She was a tiny woman with a mop of springy curls and a duffel bag nearly as big as she was strapped across her back. She dropped it onto the bed beside mine and grabbed her hips with both hands. "Aren't you that Novak puke who was nearly coffin-locked for offending one of the duke's guests?"

"No. Who told you that?" Mic scoffed, but the strain in his jaw gave him away.

"Yeah, that was definitely you," the woman said, squinting at him. "Luckily, my sire is the forgiving sort. Unless you want to consider him sending me here as retribution."

Mic looked from the woman to me as if deciding just how many enemies he wanted to end up sharing a room with. Finally, he stepped away from my bed and sulked back to his own in the far corner.

"I'm Sonja," the new vamp said, reaching out to shake my hand. "House Starling." Before I got the crazy notion that we might become friends, she added. "Stay out of my way, and I'll stay out of yours." It was a better offer than I'd had so far.

"Deal."

She nodded and settled on the opposite side of her bunk, giving me her back as she unlaced her boots and put her things away in the safe under her shelf.

My watch vibrated. *Fifteen minutes.*

No one else seemed to need the reminder. Soon, their backs lay as flat as mine against their mattresses. The familiar tug of dawn pulled at my eyelids, and just before they closed, the overhead light winked out.

"Sweet dreams, green fang," Blair's jerk sidekick whispered in the dark. "You'll learn your place soon enough."

The threat tightened my gut. I opened my mouth to shoot something hateful back at him, but day broke. Though I couldn't see the light, I felt it suck my consciousness into that strange abyss where it awaited nightfall.

Maybe I'd have a better comeback by then. Telling a vampire to bite me just didn't have the same effect as it did with human asshats.

Chapter Six

I'm dying. It was the only thought my brain could latch on to, and it pounded against my skull like a trapped animal, growing more frantic by the second. *I'm dying, I'm dying, I'm dying.*

I was conscious before the sun had fully set Sunday night. I couldn't move or see anything, but I felt the world crush in around me. I felt my body ache and my muscles scream for release like a moth straining to break free of its cocoon. It was a desperate effort that I couldn't remember ever taking hold of me this way before.

Hold on, Jenna. Roman's voice echoed in my mind, and my eyes flashed open. A suffocating darkness greeted me, and my first breath of the night was strangled as I rasped in a mouthful of icy water. I gasped and gagged as the water ripped its way back up my throat.

My hands groped for something—anything—but I found only raw wood encasing me on all sides. I was in a box. No, a cheap *coffin,* I realized as my blood vision kicked in. A cheap, *sinking* coffin, if the water rising up around me were anything to go by.

Son of a bitch.

My brain fired up with the hopeless chanting again. *I'm dying, I'm dying, I'm dying.*

And again, Roman's voice tried to soothe me. *Hold on.*

Hold on to what? I thought, irritation raking my insides and boiling my terror into outrage.

The water filled my ears, and I screamed. In the tiny box, the sound didn't travel far, but I kept screaming, refusing to let up until my throat was raw and my ears rang.

I tried to pull my knees up to my chest, but there wasn't enough room. I pressed my palms into the panel in front of my face, pushing for all I was worth. The wet wood creaked but refused to give, and the water flooded in faster.

I let out a defeated sob, but just a brief one before pinching my lips shut. Only a few inches of air remained in the box. My limbs were already freezing up, the icy water rendering my movements sluggish and weak. I pounded my fists and kicked my heels. Then I took a deep breath as the last of the air vanished.

"Hold on, Jenna!" Someone else was screaming at me now. This time, it wasn't just in my head. Mandy's frantic voice cut through the water, sounding muffled and far away.

I didn't dare open my mouth to answer her. The water was already working its way in through my nose, trickling down the back of my throat. As soon as it reached my stomach, my body spasmed, and my muscles labored to force it back up. But opening my mouth to vomit up the watery bile just let more in, and I was soon repeating the horrific act with mounting violence and panic.

My skull knocked the inside of the coffin as it was pitched to one side, and I felt gravity pull at my feet until they pressed into the end of the box. I was being moved. The water buffered the clumsy journey, but only slightly, and my heaving seizure did little to help. The rough wood snagged on my clothes and left splinters in my hands and feet.

A final, jarring *thunk* sounded, and then there was air in the box again, reappearing an inch at a time, until the lid of the coffin was ripped free. Hands plunged into the water and yanked me upright.

Kai, Mandy, and Collins loomed over me. Their fingers dug into my arms and legs as they tried to help me up and out, but I stumbled, tipping it over instead. I spilled from the box rather than exiting, landing right on the gritty floor. We were at the edge of the cave pool on the far end of the base.

Someone I didn't recognize appeared with a towel and handed it off to Kai. He wrapped it around my shoulders and sighed.

"Let the pranks begin."

"You call this a prank?" Collins bared his teeth at the dismissive remark, while Mandy squeezed my hand until my knuckles popped. The strap of her watch grazed my thigh where a splinter had taken hold, and I winced as I coughed and hacked up more water.

"This is bullshit." Her words came out laced with a growl,

and her eyes had taken on a golden hue. "Do you know who did this?"

"Mic," I rasped, ready to claw my way through hell to find the bastard.

Kai grabbed my shoulders and pulled me around to face him. "Novak didn't rise any sooner than you or I did, and he's the only recruit here from his household. He didn't even bring personal blood donors."

That left only one alternative. My blood vision throbbed painfully, and my bones ached for revenge. I stared across the cave to where Blair lingered near the opposite end of the pool, watching me with a satisfied smirk. Three men stood around her, one of them the guy from the harem. The other two were also human. I could tell from the wash of red painting their features.

They would burn for this. I didn't care how affluent or above the law they thought they were. I would find a way to collect my pound of flesh.

"How did you find me?" I asked Kai, pulling the towel tighter around my shoulders. My hair dripped in my face, and a tremor reverberated through my chest. I couldn't be sure if it was from the cold or the desperate wrath I was keeping caged in there.

"Roman," Kai answered under his breath. I could feel his eyes measuring me, taking note of my condition as much as my tunnel vision and what it was focused on. "I guess your blood hasn't quite made it out of his system. You got lucky."

"And them? Are they lucky, too?" I asked through clenched teeth.

His hand squeezed my shoulder tighter. "Without hard evidence, accusations only lead to more trouble," he said.

"If this were *real* boot camp, someone would be getting their ass kicked out of here for this," Collins said, glaring up as the program sergeants approached. It was the wrong thing to say.

"You want *real* boot camp?" the white-haired sergeant over the human program spat at Collins. "Get in formation, or I'll be kicking *your* ass out of here."

Collins gritted his teeth, but I eased his hand off my arm. "I'll be fine. Go."

"You, too," Sergeant Carmichael said to Mandy next. The girl was even more reluctant to leave me, but I waved her off as I had Collins.

The remaining sergeant had to be Faye Sorano. Her stony face held that perfect alert vacancy that Vanessa and Roman were so good at, but the similarities ended there. Her military cap fit snuggly, and the bit of hair I could see was dark and pixie short. She walked with purpose, chest lifted and hands folded behind her back.

Mandy squeezed my arm again, and I patted her hand.

"I'm seriously going to be fine. I'll feel better after I feed."

Sergeant Sorano cut in with an insult to add to my injury. "First meal isn't until midnight, cadet. Your enemies won't wait until you've fed and feel better." She scoffed at my grimace. "Sunset to midnight is the busiest shift for most Blood Vice agents. Our job here is to make sure you're trained to handle yourself at a moment's notice while keeping your bloodlust under control."

"I'll just go change then." I stood and peeled off the wet towel Kai had draped over my shoulders. He took it from me with a tight smile, as if he knew my night would only get worse from here.

"That can wait, too," Sorano said. "Afraid you've used up too much time as it is."

"What?" I looked down at my wet clothes and bare feet before scowling at her.

"Get in line or go home." She turned and marched off toward the vampire barracks where the rest of the vamp cadets were lining up outside, completely unfazed by my near-death experience.

To be fair, I wasn't entirely sure a vampire could drown. But it had been *really* fucking unpleasant. And a quick bite would have made me feel better. Dry clothes, too. Or simply breaking Blair's upturned nose. The image gave me the strength to take the first step in her direction.

I was going to pass this course, or I would die trying. The latter seemed more likely at this point.

Despite Kai's good advice, I was the last cadet in line, taking up the empty spot beside Sonja. Sergeant Sorano didn't seem surprised. Neither did anyone else. Even if Mic weren't responsible, he sure seemed willing to take credit for my close call. He stood to Sonja's left and leaned back just enough to ogle me with a hateful sneer.

"Have a nice swim, green fang?" he whispered.

"Eyes up here," Sorano snapped, drawing our attention ahead.

Six stacks of folded, black fatigues waited on the table. Before each stack rested a pair of boots and a black watch. Paper name cards indicated who each set of gear belonged to.

Sergeant Sorano stood behind the table. "Gather your things, go change, and meet back here in ten minutes." She glanced down at her watch, taking note of the time. "The last person to return will be running an extra mile today."

And everyone was suddenly in motion, shoving past one another to collect their gear. I waited for the others to clear the table, and once they'd filtered through the barracks' entrance, I stripped out of my soaked clothes. I disposed of them in a trash barrel next to the table before pulling on the remaining stack of fatigues.

Sergeant Sorano watched me with the closest thing I'd

seen to a smile on her face. Impressing her couldn't hurt, but more than that, I wasn't interested in running an extra mile. Not today, Satan.

My bra and underwear were damp, but I'd survive. I slipped on the black boots and quickly laced them up. Then I buckled the watch around my wrist. I was back in line before the next dressed recruit emerged from the barracks.

Blair glowered at me as she took her place. The other four cadets followed soon after her, the last one being her spiteful sidekick.

"Novak," Sergeant Sorano called. "Congratulations, you'll be running nine miles today instead of eight."

He huffed an indignant sound. "But I came out at the same time as everyone else." His eyes migrated to me, and he frowned.

"Ten miles, Novak," Sorano snapped. "Unless you have anything else to say?"

He threw up his hands in surrender and took his spot in line between Blair and Sonja.

After we'd stood for an uncomfortably long time with the sergeant pacing in front of us, staring us down with her lethal gaze, she finally addressed us by holding up her arm and tapping the face of the watch on her wrist.

"These watches are now your keepers. They will track where you go at all times while you're inside this facility," she said, making eye contact with us one by one. She paused a bit longer on Blair, until the catty vampire's cheeks colored, and then she moved on down the line. "They will open the doors to the crypt and harem, and clock your time when you train. They are waterproof. You will not take them off for any reason whatsoever. If you do, you will be discharged from this program. Do you understand?"

"Yes, ma'am," we answered in unison.

I stood up taller as some of the dread dissipated from my psyche. This would make things significantly harder for the bitch's human goons to screw with me during the day.

Now if I could just keep House Novak's pit bull from pissing on my bunk or chewing up my boots, I'd have it made.

Chapter Seven

My first week in the bat cave was…lonely. Kai had been right about how little I would get to see Mandy and Collins. Our paths crossed twice, and I do mean crossed.

The split-second encounter with Mandy had been just enough time for a high-five. Her optimistic smile led me to believe she was getting on better with her training than Collins—who merely grimaced in my direction as he exited the obstacle course the one time I'd spotted him. Of course, with all the mud in his eyes and matted in his hair, I couldn't be sure he'd seen me at all.

The cadets in my own unit kept their distance. After the incident with the cave pool, no one was eager to draw the ire of whoever was gunning for me. And though the culprit was plenty obvious, none of the officials wanted to point fingers without concrete evidence—certainly not at such a noble, respected house. So, I was on my own.

Since we were at the mercy of the sun, even this far underground, our schedule actually lengthened by a few minutes every day. The fancy watches we'd been issued were calibrated to count down the first twenty minutes after sunset, at which time we were expected to be lined up in front of the cave pool—where I'd nearly drowned.

After running eight miles, it was on to the obstacle course, climbing rock walls and ledges, crawling through mud, doing hundreds of pushups, sit-ups, and pull-ups. And then swimming across that damned pool. The bathing suit Laura had suggested stayed in my bag. We were expected to swim the distance in full gear while wearing concrete-filled backpacks. Only then were we allowed to shower and have our first meal.

The intensity of the training was such that we were expected to eat twice a day. I had to get used to my adopted harem rather quickly, feeding from the four humans in careful rotation. The days I had Natalie and Sampson were my favorite, and I'd often linger in the harem to visit with them about their otherwise normal lives and the airport drama that circulated through the terminal café where several of them worked part-time.

Kai's law class began at 2:00 A.M., and at 4:00 A.M. we had combat training. For now, that meant hand-to-hand defense and arrest tactics, but as the weeks progressed, we'd be moving on to firearms. Sergeant Sorano kept a closer eye on me during the sessions in the sparring ring, though I couldn't be sure if it was more for my protection or Blair's.

We were neck and neck, always a hairsbreadth away from mauling each other. The redhead had been through some martial arts training. I could tell by the way she moved—like a ninja ballerina catapulted up from the depths of Hell. And while she'd been a vampire a few decades longer than I had, my advantage lay in the fact that I had real-world experience. Practical training, thanks to the police academy and seven years on the streets of St. Louis. At least, that's what I chalked up my resilience to, rather than confess my regal lineage. It was slowly killing me that I couldn't rub my pedigree in her smug face. Oh, how I wanted to.

Mic was another story. He came at me hard and fast, twisting my arm up behind my back or planting my face on the ground within seconds every time. And he never called me by name, opting instead for *vampling* or *green fang*. The other three cadets were more of a mixed bag. Sometimes, I won. Sometimes, I lost. It was just the way of things. But I never, *ever* laid down for Blair. And she never laid down for me. Sorano would eventually grow bored of our uneasy stalemate and force us to persist until one or the other yielded, but until she did, we'd continue to play this game.

By the time Sunday rolled around and I was granted my first phone break, I was desperate to hear a friendly voice. So, for the life of me, I don't know why my fingers instantly dialed Roman's number. He answered on the second ring.

"Are you okay?" My heart thrummed at the concern in his voice.

"Yeah, I am," I said. "Thanks to you." I leaned against the side wall of the phone booth and pulled my legs up onto the seat beside me.

Roman released a tense breath. "I called Kai the second I…felt you."

"Yeah, about that…" Where did I even begin? "Are we like, telepathically linked now or something?"

"It's temporary," he said as if the thought relieved him. "And it's probably already worn off by now. Hopefully." *Hopefully?* Regret tightened my stomach, and I swallowed.

"Is that the only time you've *felt* me?"

He was quiet for a few seconds. I couldn't tell if he was carefully considering the question or debating whether or not he wanted to answer. "Yes," he said tightly.

"Good. Thanks," I said again, feeling my face warm as my mind went blank and my tongue numb.

"You're welcome."

How many times had I wished that our conversation after I'd saved his life had gone this way? I pictured his pained expression, the way his fingers had squeezed the steering wheel right before he confessed that he wished I had let him die. That he would have risen as a vampire and been pardoned the remaining years on his contract.

The silence stretched for a moment before he cleared his throat again. "Was there…something else you called about?"

"No, I just wanted to thank you," I blurted. "That's all. It's been a long week, and this is the first time I've been allowed to use the phone…" My voice trailed off.

"Oh." He sounded about as uncomfortable as I felt. This polite middle ground wasn't a place we were used to meeting each other.

"Well, then." I took a deep breath. "I'll let you go."

"Jenna?" My shoulders trembled at the sound of my name on his lips.

"Yeah, Roman?"

"*Puedes hacerlo.*"

I grinned and pressed my chin into the palm of my free hand. "*Gracias.*"

With butterflies still swarming my stomach, I called to check in with Vin next.

"God, Jenna." He hissed out an angry sigh. "I've been worried sick. I've left, like, a hundred voicemails. I was about to get in my car and drive to Denver."

"There's no cell service here, Vin. I told you that." Annoyance stirred in my gut, and I waited for the usual tinge of guilt to dilute it. "I'm sorry," I said in a more gentle voice. "Everything is fine. This is just the first time I've been allowed to use the phone. The training is pretty intense, so…"

"But you're okay?" His tone downshifted with mine, sounding more meek and weepy.

"Absolutely." There was no sense in telling him about the pool fiasco. He'd be a bigger wreck over it than I was. "I have to go."

"When will I hear from you again?" he asked.

"Maybe in a few weeks? I don't really know." I suppressed a groan.

"Okay." The dejected pout in his voice grated on me when it should have melted my heart. At least, a little. I was steeling myself for what was to come, and that preparation felt selfish, as if I were dragging this out for my benefit and wasting Vin's time. But I couldn't bring myself to cut him loose just yet.

"Talk to you soon," I said and hung up before I changed my mind.

My last call went to Laura, though I knew she wouldn't answer. Filming was keeping her busy all hours of the day and night. I left her a quick message, letting her know that I was alive and that training was underway and going well. I left off the grittier details for her sake, too.

The single phone booth was set up near the base tunnel entrance. It was a five-minute walk from the vampire barracks. On my way back, I ran into Mandy and Collins. They'd been waiting for me at a picnic table set up in front of the cafeteria building situated halfway between the human and CAT barracks.

Mandy reclined on the edge of the table, her booted ankles crossed on the bench below. She wore a pair of the black fatigue pants everyone had been issued, paired with a black tank top. Her hair was pulled back into a French braid. It was how I'd kept my own hair all week, too.

Collins sat on the bench beside Mandy's feet, wearing a long-sleeved, black undershirt like mine. He was hunched over, elbows on his knees and fingers laced together. A bruise circled the apple of his left cheek, and a tiny cut marred his chin. It wasn't an unexpected sight, considering the training exercises, but I did feel sorry that he wasn't able to heal as quickly as the vamp cadets. I'd had a black eye just yesterday, thanks to Mic, but after feeding, it was a distant memory.

Beyond the superficial bumps and scrapes, Collins looked ragged, like maybe he hadn't slept well since we arrived. I wondered if the beds in his barracks were as cozy as the ones in mine. Then I wondered if maybe he was enjoying Blair's half-sired compadre as much as I was enjoying her.

Cain Davis. He'd been one of the three men standing at the pool with her after I'd been hauled out of the water. The two others were run-of-the-mill humans, personal members of the House Hanson harem. Gavin and Omar. They didn't even make eye contact with me in the barracks' harem. Not since that first day. But Cain…

There was something about the way the half-sired looked at me that made my skin crawl. His pale gray eyes were unsettling enough as it was, but added to his ghostly complexion and the long, white hair he kept pulled back in a low ponytail, he was downright spooky.

I stopped in front of the picnic table, and Mandy threw herself at me, her arms squeezing around my neck in a bone-crushing hug.

"I get to go camping in the woods with a real pack next full moon," she squealed in my ear.

Collins rolled his eyes. "They'll probably sniff each other's butts and everything."

Mandy let me go so she could slug him in the arm. "You're just jealous."

"I am," he said. "Happy? Now quit rubbing it in my face."

I glanced down at my watch. "I have to be in class in ten minutes, so give me the shorthand version of your first week."

Mandy ticked off her highlights on the fingers of one hand. "The wolf division of Blood Vice is referred to as the Cadaver Dogs. I'll be initiated into their pack once training is done. I still get to work with you and Mr. Poutypants here afterwards, and this has been the best week of my life," she finished in a single breath.

Collins stared at her and swallowed hard as I looked to him. "Maybe I should have let her bite me instead of bleeding for you."

I winced apologetically. "If it makes you feel any better, my week hasn't been so great either."

"Someone tried to drown you." He snorted. "So I should

think not."

"I wish we could all go camping together," Mandy said, more to herself than to us. A dreamy haze clouded her eyes. "There are some really great spots the girls in Spero Heights have told me about."

"Maybe when we get back." I gave her shoulder a squeeze and turned to Collins again, expectantly. He sighed and ticked off his highlights with less enthusiasm than Mandy had.

"The half-sired assfaces should have their own program. Humans are apparently self-sufficient chattel. I miss the sun. I miss my husband. This job better be fucking worth it."

"Yeah." I nodded. "I guess I should head to class."

"Wait, what about you?" Mandy asked, grabbing my arm before I could leave. "We deserve a rundown, too, you know."

"Right." I grimaced, knowing the only pleasant thing I could share with them would probably go over as well as my snack time with Stella had. "Nobody likes me. Everybody hates me. Guess I'll go eat worms."

Mandy's cheeks puffed out as she blew a raspberry at me. I skipped back a step before she could slug my arm like she had Collins and winked at her.

"I'll catch up with you guys later," I called over my shoulder. "Hang in there. We can do this."

I believed it, too.

Because so did Roman.

Chapter Eight

The lengthening nights in the bat cave were relentless, but as the minutes accrued on our training sessions, they also drew out our harem breaks. And each time I met with Natalie, I picked up something new. Our visits were even more illuminating than Kai's law classes.

From Sergeant Sorano addressing the cadets, I learned that the two mystery vampires in my unit were named Emma and Andre, from House Kincade and House Freeman. And from the bits of gossip I'd gathered in the harem, I quickly discerned the pecking order of the households currently training on base.

I was disappointed to discover that House Zajalvo was barely a blip on the radar. Of course, that wasn't much of a shocker, considering the way I'd been treated so far. I'd wanted to believe my orphan status was to blame, but Zajalvo had been a reclusive and modest vampire. There were no others in his household, and he wasn't a member of the Vampiric High Council—the supreme court of supernatural society that Roman had briefly mentioned in his notes.

Cadets like Blair, Mic, and Sonja came from families with a dozen or more vampires to their name. And while they were higher-ranking households, the three recruits were low on the scion totem pole at home. For them, training to join Blood

Vice was like a rite of passage—a hurdle they needed to cross if they wanted to advance within the family hierarchy. Each household with a seat on the high council was expected to pledge at least one scion to Blood Vice every century.

The lowbred vampire houses without council seats, like those Andre and Emma were from, were not required to supply Blood Vice with fresh recruits, but many of them did for the simple fact that it provided discipline for restless scions and a steady, decent paycheck to help support their households.

I was in a category of my very own. The last member of a lowbred house. A runt. Easy fodder for the aggressive, entitled shits in my unit. Those playing center field were probably relieved that I was there to take the heat off their backs.

The distance between our respective houses was made even more apparent in Kai's law class. The upper-crust vamps were given leniency and privileges. Slights against them were taken seriously, while affronts they committed against lesser households were often overlooked. *No shit,* I thought at the unjust reveal, wondering what would've happened had *I* prearranged a watery grave for *Blair* instead of the other way around.

The same biased treatment wasn't so uncommon in human law, but they didn't stack the deck beforehand by spelling it out in their judicial texts. Humans at least *tried* to pretend that we were all equal and should be treated fairly, even if they didn't always practice what they preached.

The clear disadvantage of me having *zero* knowledge concerning vampire legislature made Kai's class hard to follow. The other cadets were annoyed by my ignorance and constant interruptions, and since the textbook we were working from only covered the *what* of the law, I was left with a whole lot of *why?*

"The library is just north of the training course," Kai finally told me after class one night. "Some of the human program texts might be easier for you to grasp. Alice, the librarian, should be able to point you in the right direction."

The *human* program texts? He'd said it as if he were directing me back to preschool.

I swallowed the angry lump in my throat and nodded. "I'll check it out. Thanks."

After having my ass handed to me by Mic in combat training, I headed to the harem. My second scheduled feeding of the night was with Ned. His room smelled like jet fuel, likely from his daytime job as an airport baggage handler. He was a stout human with beady eyes and dry skin, and while he wasn't as charming as the others, he was polite. Like Natalie, he was here mostly to collect a check, but bleeding in the bat cave also helped with his medical condition, polycythemia vera, or thick blood disease. Why pay a doctor to perform a medieval bloodletting when there were perfectly good bloodsuckers willing to pay a patient for the honor?

Ned's thick blood didn't bother me, but his apathetic silence was a bit unnerving. He was my least favorite of the donors. Still, I offered up an apology for cutting our visit short. I wasn't one for fast food, but he didn't seem to mind. He gave a half-hearted wave and snatched up a hotrod magazine from the corner of his dresser as I left.

September was almost over, and with it, week three of training. *Nine weeks to go,* I reminded myself as I walked across the base toward the library. Like all the other buildings in the bat cave, it was unmarked and made of concrete. The amount of gray in the place was depressing—only redeemed by the gaping cave mouth with its crystal-crusted walls.

The sight of the pool no longer sent a thrill of panic through me. In fact, the spot of color seemed to brighten my mood, much like Natalie's rainbow presence, even when Mic taunted me as we completed our nightly swim with the other cadets.

"Is it nap time, green fang?"

"Looks like your waterbed sprang a leak."

"Thirsty, little vampling?"

Blair only snickered, letting the creep take credit for her *prank.*

Nine weeks, I repeated in my mind as I passed the cave

mouth and pool. To my right, the obstacle course sprawled across a good quarter of the bat cave. It was the size of a football field and followed a lap pattern around the inside of the running track. The bland, cookie-cutter edifices crowded in on the other three sides of the course. I headed for the northernmost end as Kai had instructed.

The building that housed the library was two stories tall. I found Alice behind a small desk on the first floor. The open room was crammed floor-to-ceiling with books and several study tables partitioned off by towering shelves. Rather than industrial overhead lights like I'd seen everywhere else in the bat cave, orbed pendant lights glowed softly over the stacks. All the furniture in the library was made of actual wood. I stood in the center of the room, gawking as I turned in a wide circle until Alice tapped her long nails on her desk.

"Can I help you find something, dear?" She gave me a tight smile.

"I'm looking for a textbook…"

"The intermediate vampire law books are—"

"No. Actually…" I bit my lip and blushed. "I'm looking for a book from the human program?" I said, my sentence hitching at the end as if in question.

"Oh." Alice's face fell into a neutral mask. "That corner." She pointed a finger without removing her eyes from me. I nodded my thanks and hurried out of her sight like a cockroach taking cover.

Sunrise was an hour off, so I tried to make the most of my time, quickly piling books onto an empty table. I hated to admit it, but Kai was right. The human program editions were easier for me to digest. Maybe because I'd been one just a few months ago. In a way, I still thought of myself in that context.

The information was essentially the same, though it was presented in a less demeaning way toward humans, and it did a better job of stressing the importance of the hemoarchy, which seemed to be such common knowledge among vampires that Kai's class didn't even cover it.

The vampire family on top, House Lilith, was a European transplant sent to the New World with the early pilgrims. They oversaw the immigration of other vampires, noble and lowbred alike, and eventually founded the Vampiric High Council whose steadfast rule began even before the American Revolution.

Humans in the know were expected to recognize vampires as the superior species. It was hard to wrap my mind around—this idea that I'd died and risen as a completely different species. The test results from the blood I'd let Vin take didn't really leave any room for doubt, though.

The vampire relationships were better outlined for the human program, too. There were distinct differences between how a *proper* vampire should conduct themselves with a harem donor versus a half-sired donor. I'd had an inkling of how things worked, but seeing it on the page felt like learning what sex was all about in health class. I pulled the book closer and cupped my cheeks with both hands, letting my cool fingers sooth my shame.

The table rocked, and I glanced up to find Mic's boot propped on the edge of the far end, a shit-eating grin splayed across his hateful face. "You should be spending your free time on the course," he said. "Unless you'd rather be a neutered brain fang like Natani than a Blood Vice agent."

I rested my arms over the open pages before me, hoping he wouldn't take any interest in my reading selection. I really didn't need to give him anything else to torture me with.

"Mr. Novak," Alice called from the front desk. She gave his boot a pointed look. "Respect the library furnishings, and keep your voice down."

He sneered at her but obeyed, letting his boot drop to the library floor before turning back to me. "You're not even in the right section. These nursery rhymes are for the humans. Do you really think you're going to pass the finals and be accepted onto Blood Vice?"

"What's your problem?" I hissed under my breath for fear that Alice would reprimand me next. "Why can't you leave me alone?"

"Yeah, Novak. What's with the stalker routine?" Sonja

appeared behind him, and his shoulders squared. He'd already crossed House Starling once and, apparently, his punishment had been severe enough to make him think twice about trying it again.

"This isn't your business." Mic's square jaw flexed, and his fingers curled into fists at his sides.

"Shouldn't you be saving all that charm for a human donor?" Sonja asked, turning away from us to skim her fingers along a shelf.

Mic jerked his chin in my direction. "This one's so green, it's hard to tell her apart from them."

"Ah, here we are," Sonja said, sliding a thick book free. She turned it around to show him the cover. *The Willful Scion & Discipline in the 20th Century.*

I didn't understand the significance until Mic blanched. He made a choking noise in the back of his throat and coughed into one of his closed fists, glaring at Sonja. What had happened to him after he insulted House Starling? I wondered.

"Oh." Sonja pointed a finger at the corner of her mouth. "You got a little something there. Is that blood?" Mic wiped at his mouth, but then Sonja gasped. "No, I think it must be Blair's shit from all that ass-kissing you've been doing. Tell me, are you two planning for a winter wedding? Because I'm pretty sure her sire planned on tapping that for another decade or two, so…"

Mic's fangs snapped out, and I almost toppled out of my chair. Vile as he was, the bastard could move. His eyes dilated, and the skin around his mouth stretched and creased as he hissed at Sonja.

"Mr. Novak," Alice said again, her voice low and aggravated. "This is a library. You will conduct yourself as such or study elsewhere."

Mic panted murderously, but before Sonja could goad him into complete ruin, he was gone. Zipping right out of the building. His wake stirred the pages of the books on my table. I reached out to stop them, but I was too late.

Sonja chuckled and put her own book back on the shelf before taking a seat across the table from me. "He's really so fragile," she said. "It doesn't take much to send him on his way."

"That's a neat trick." I smiled at her. "I wish I had time to learn it."

Sonja nodded and glanced down at my collection of books. "Yeah, you've definitely got enough on your plate for now." Her mouth twisted to one side, and she fingered one of her springy curls. "Don't hate me for asking the same question, but I am curious. Do you really think you're going to pass the finals and be accepted onto Blood Vice?"

I closed the book in front of me and sighed. "I don't

know.”

“Then why put yourself through this?” I’d asked myself the same question a million times before.

“My harem is depending on me. I have to try.” My eyelids felt heavy. I closed another book and began stacking them in a pile to put back on the shelf. “Why are you here?” I asked, wondering if maybe she really had been sent just to torture Mic. She was so good at it.

“It was either this or medical school again.” Sonja huffed and rolled her eyes. “My first degree was earned as a half-sired. Any idea how long it takes to get that kind of degree via night school?”

I blinked at her. “Vampires attend human universities?”

“Don’t look so surprised. Vampires are in just about every industry out there. Of course they go to college.”

“Why medical school?” I asked.

“It’s what House Starling is known for.” She lifted an eyebrow and pursed her lips. “Plucked you right out of the grave, didn’t they? It’s all right,” she added when my face fell. “We all start somewhere.”

“But doctors deal with so much…blood.” I crinkled my nose. “Seems awfully risky.”

“That’s a fair point.” Sonja nodded and pulled one leg up, propping her thigh against the arm of her chair. She picked at a loose string on her fatigue pants. “The bloodlust isn’t so bad after the first decade, and human doctors can be…problematic. They poke and prod where they shouldn't sometimes, even the ones who've been accepted into the fold. That's why House Starling runs our very own lab, too."

I thought of my arrangement with Vin and shifted uncomfortably in my seat. His research would definitely have to be terminated. The conversation wasn't one I was looking forward to.

Sonja ignored my aura of guilt and went on. "Healthy harems need regular checkups, and even half-sireds are not totally immune to disease or injury. If their potential sires don't feed them well enough, the repercussions can be devastating. Cain, for instance."

My ears pricked at the name of Blair's *numero uno* flunky. "What do you mean?"

Sonja gave me a disdainful sigh. "The white hair? The washed-out irises? That generally doesn't happen unless a half-sired has been deprived of blood at one point or another."

I thought of Roman's white hair and his icy blues. Before our most recent falling out, he'd told me that he'd been assigned to three different vampires over the past fifty years. Had he missed feedings during those transitions?

Sonja shrugged at my horrified expression. "Our blood doesn't fully root itself in a circulatory system unless the heart stops pumping for at least six hours. The lungs, kidneys, and liver are pretty efficient organs, and once they filter out the anti-aging molecules of vampire blood, which can take anywhere from five to eight days, a human body's age catches up with them rather quickly."

Vin would have had a field day with all of this new information. I'd made up my mind that I wouldn't be sharing it with him. It would just complicate things. And I was already fretting over what he'd discovered that had him in such a secretive fluster with me on the phone lately.

Sonja glanced down at her watch and sighed. "Welp, baby fangs, I'll catch you back at the crypt. The sun waits for no one."

"Thanks," I said, standing up from the table at the same time she did. "I really appreciate you scaring Mic off."

Sonja grinned. "Don't thank me for that. I chose the same training session as Novak so I'd have plenty of entertainment if things got boring around here." She gave me a two-fingered salute and left me in the library to replace my books.

Maybe Roman's advice to not make friends had exceptions. Sonja seemed like a pretty good candidate to me.

Chapter Nine

Several days later, Mandy, Sergeant Carmichael, and a young, male werewolf—the only other recruit training in Mandy's unit—were packed into Kai's golf cart. The shrill of the electric engine cut through the sounds of my unit splashing across the cave pool. My mind painted a comical picture as it parked along the uneven edge where the cave mouth began. I imagined what might happen if the wolves all exited the vehicle before Kai. Would it tip over? The vampire easily weighed more than all of them put together.

I finished my last lap and pulled myself up onto the edge of the pool, shrugging off the concrete backpack. My shoulders screamed, but I ignored the burn seizing up my spine and stood to towel-dry my face and hair.

Sergeant Sorano's back was to me as she exchanged a few words with Sergeant Carmichael and Kai. I slipped up slowly, snagging Mandy's attention. The girl scrambled out of the cart before either sergeant could say anything and threw her arms around my neck, ignoring my soaked fatigues.

Mandy was actually wearing her full uniform for a change. As we hugged, I realized she was also wearing a thicker coat under her jacket. I spotted the duffel bags stacked in back of the cart, and my heart sank. They were leaving for the full moon camping trip.

"We'll be gone for three days," she whispered against my neck. "Somewhere in the Rockies."

"Starsgard," Carmichael barked. "This isn't a slumber party."

"Yes, ma'am," Mandy said, pushing away from me and climbing back inside the golf cart.

Sergeant Sorano scowled and glanced over my shoulder to where the others were just finishing up in the cave pool. I had my weaknesses as a vampling, but I was discovering that that didn't mean I was completely devoid of strengths. I even swam faster than Mic, who always bested me on the track and in hand-to-hand.

"Hit the showers, Skye," Sorano said, having nothing worse to shout at me.

"Yes, ma'am." I shot Mandy one last smile. "See you when you get back." Then I eyeballed the boy in her unit, as if I could tell his intentions with a glance. Most villains weren't as transparent as Mic or Blair, unfortunately.

Mandy was tough and could hold her own, and I doubted she'd seem so giddy over the trip if she had concerns about this boy. Still, I considered her my responsibility and worried about her safety and well-being. Just where, exactly, *up in the Rockies* were they going? How far would they be from civilization? From a hospital? My muscles twitched anxiously as I watched the golf cart speed off toward the tunnel exit at the other side of the base.

Sorano gave me another scowl that sent me turning on my heels and heading off for the barracks and the shower that I badly needed. My first feeding was with Natalie tonight, and I wanted to quiz her on how much she knew about more…*involved* vampire relationships than the one we shared.

My library findings were growing curiouser and curiouser. They were driving me to distraction. While I should have been studying more of the day-to-day laws that were frequently violated, I'd lost myself in books about vampire physiology, culture, and history. It was fascinating. I was already debating how I might be able to sneak a book or two out with me after training was over. I was too mortified by the idea of Mic or Blair discovering my notes to take any. I would have loved to snap pictures of a few of the pages, but my phone had died my third night on base, and there were no charging outlets in the crypt, or anywhere on base that I'd seen.

The showers were co-ed, but the large stalls were divided by more concrete, and if Mic had the audacity to harass me there, there wasn't a family fancy enough to keep me from digging out his eyeballs. It might not kill him, but thanks to a few more awkward library sessions with Sonja, I now knew that he definitely wouldn't be growing a new pair if I relieved him of those—or any other assets.

Sonja's medical predisposition clarified a lot of the

seemingly mystical elements of vampirism that I read about in the outdated volumes. For all of their perceived superiority, vampires had used magic to explain away science they didn't yet understand—the same as humans.

Most donors enjoyed being bitten because a chemical compound in vampire saliva triggered the release of endorphins in the human body. And treating internal silver damage with the "blood of one's enemy" worked because of a special, healing enzyme produced in vampire blood as they neared true death—any dying vampire's blood would do, but why drain a friend when you could drain a foe?

My rudimentary vampire education was rough-going. Often, I felt as if I were trapped under an avalanche of outdated textbooks that had all been proven at least half-false. Sonja helped weed out the junk and pointed me toward volumes with fresher facts once she tired of answering my questions herself.

After my shower, I left my dirty fatigues in the hamper inside the washroom. A few of the harem staff washed the cadets' clothing and did basic housecleaning duties around the base. Each of the human donors employed at the bat cave had some sort of part-time job closely linked to their blood work. Some of them were baristas in a terminal café owned by House Lilith, which supplied the human, half-sired, and wolf guests on base with their meals. Some worked in security or baggage, transporting luggage trailers back and forth across the runway. They served as the base's eyes and ears topside.

It was all very simple and efficient, requiring minimal staff in and out of the base or airport. And there wasn't a lot of fancy technology or structural maintenance to fuss over—not with concrete walls and no Wi-Fi to speak of. There was one camera hardwired into the elevator, and the feed went to a single monitor just inside the tunnel. It was manned by a vampire and a couple of harem donors, and it had to be the easiest job on base.

On my rougher days of training, when Mic and Blair were extra harassy or I was extra lonely, I wondered how much that easy job paid. I asked myself how much would really be enough to give it all up. How long would it take before the mindless, thankless monotony of it ate me alive? Could it be worth it?

The few minutes I shared with Mandy and Collins helped keep my spirits afloat. I enjoyed my time with Natalie, too, but our friendship was stunted by our working relationship. We both knew I'd be leaving the bat cave in a couple of months, and she'd be staying several months longer before going off to college. That was the arrangement.

We all understood how this worked. But I had to keep reminding myself that she wasn't *mine*. She wasn't a member of my blood harem. I wouldn't be taking her with me when I left. Which meant that I would be resigned to drinking blood out of a paper cup again, especially if I ended things with Vin the way I planned to.

I had to hope that joining Blood Vice, and finally being accepted into the fold of the community, would grant me better insight and resources. Maybe there was a bulletin board in Roman's field office—the one I expected to be hired at in St. Louis—that occasionally had flyers with those little tear-off phone numbers for human donors looking to join an exclusive harem. Maybe one of my new colleagues would know a guy. Who knew?

Sonja had also given me a quick lowdown on the Who's Who of supernatural society. A little vamp pop culture preview—the famous artists and musicians of the underground as well as the richest and most elite households. While entertaining, I somehow doubted I'd cross paths with any of those affluent vamps in Blood Vice.

Most of the fancypants houses were headed up by fat bats that ran some company or another. House Hanson was known for their network security software engineers, the same way House Starling was known for their doctors. And House Novak was, of all things, known for their *haute couture*. They made sure the fancy vamps were always dressed to kill.

Mic just didn't have what it took to be a true fashionista. His hateful face was probably pretty enough when he was sleeping—but Sonja mentioned that he'd botched a few co-logne commercials before finally being shipped off to join Blood Vice. I guessed it was easy to torment me when he knew I wouldn't have all of this juicy dirt on him as a vampling. I hadn't sprung it on him yet, but I would eventually. I was just waiting for the right moment. I'd only have the element of surprise once. It needed to count.

I also learned a bit about Vanessa. I tried not to seem too interested when Sonja spoke about House Sorano, hoping my curiosity struck the right balance between wanting to learn and being a busybody. And hoping my jealousy wasn't too obvious. I had no right to be bitter, but I also couldn't control my gut reactions.

Lord Sorano, Faye's sire, and Vanessa's grandsire, owned Sorano Munitions, the company responsible for designing and manufacturing Blood Vice's girly-colored Silver Wolfs-bane ammo. Many of House Sorano's scions went into Blood Vice and quickly climbed the ranks. Faye had become the head sergeant over the vampire training program even before siring Vanessa.

Roman's potential sire had spent five years as a member of Faye's harem on base before the sergeant was granted per-mission to half-sire her. Then she'd spent another twenty years serving alongside Faye on base before being fully turned, and another thirty before being transferred to a Blood Vice field office. She'd spent over fifty years in a hellhole I was wondering if I'd last three months in. Maybe it wasn't this *exact* hellhole, but I somehow doubted the previous bat cave had been any swankier than the upgraded one under the airport.

I was waiting for Sonja to spill some real dirt, but everything she shared about Vanessa just made me either feel sorry for her or even more inferior than I had before. And it made the femme fatale vamp's super dry, super serious personality more understandable, too. Jealousy, sympathy, and guilt were complicated enough on their own, but put them in a blender? Ugh.

Regardless of my emotional turmoil, talking with Sonja made me feel as if there might be some relatively normal future in store for me. Even if only one percent of vampires were like her and the rest were Mics and Blairs, I'd survive. I might yet learn to enjoy my new life. So far, it had felt more like survival. But while I appreciated Sonja's earnest sharing, I saved the more embarrassing blood donor relationship questions for Natalie. She could be more objective and humble about those things, since it was all so new to her, too. With Sonja, it was easier to confess not knowing a new person's backstory than it was to admit not knowing how my own damn body chemistry worked.

The harem was quiet when I arrived. My wet hair dripped on the rug that sprawled through the hallway where Natalie's room was located. The other cadets would be there soon, too, but I rarely bumped into them. We stayed in our respective donors' rooms. I'd spotted Kai in the foyer once, but never Sorano. I wondered if she kept her harem elsewhere or maybe waited until we were all in Kai's class.

A few of the bedroom doors were propped open, spilling conversation and music into the hallway. No radio or television—just battery-powered CD players or iPods that the donors probably charged up top during their day jobs. The BATC was frugal with their budget, and other than basic lighting, a well pump, and the golf cart charging dock, they didn't spend much on utilities. It was a real Stone Age setup around here.

I picked out Natalie's door, decorated with the glittery outline of a raven, and knocked. I wasn't prepared for her melodramatic greeting.

"Tom Petty's dead," she wailed, thick mascara streaking down her face. "His heart gave out, and now the Heartbreakers are finished, and I'm heartbroken."

"Oh, honey." I'd barely opened my arms before she fell into me, sobbing hysterically.

My questions about sharing lifeblood could wait. I wasn't even sure I should be feeding on her in this condition. I heard Mic's obnoxious laugh filter down the hallway from the foyer and gently nudged Natalie back into her room, closing the door behind us. *Breakdown* crooned softly from the CD player.

"Last year was dark enough with the loss of Snape and the Goblin King." She hiccupped and rubbed her wet cheek against my sleeve. I cringed, wondering how much makeup she was leaving behind. "There's going to be a vampire memorial walk down Ventura Boulevard—well." She rolled her eyes as she pulled away from me and sniffled. "Not with *real* vampires, obviously."

"Wouldn't that be a sight?" I gave her a small smile. "Do you want me to see if Sampson would be willing to trade shifts with you?"

"No, no, no." She shook her head. "I think I could use the endorphins right now anyway."

"Are you sure?" The idea of snacking on a crying girl seemed a little too…cheesy B horror film for my taste.

"Yes. Absolutely." Natalie grabbed two wet wipes from her night table and scrubbed her cheeks with them, washing away most of her muddled makeup. Then she finger-combed her frazzled, rainbow mane and sat on the edge of her bed. "Better make it quick, though," she said as *Insider* began to play, and her eyes glistened with the beginnings of fresh tears.

I snuggled in next to her as she lifted her wrist to my mouth. Thanks to the base harem donors, I was getting more comfortable with the fang-to-flesh feeding. It was no longer a blundering endeavor that I begrudgingly endured. I enjoyed myself a lot of the time, and I was beginning to find some semblance of separation in the act—discerning the different kinds of intimacy that Stella had mentioned.

My fangs settled over Natalie's wrist, and I gently pressed down until her flesh opened. Her breath shuddered as my mouth suctioned around the new lesions. I'd gotten better at this part of the process, too, causing less damage and pain. I used my tongue and fingers on the veins in her arm to stimulate blood flow. I could have just as easily bitten down harder to get things moving along, but that method was for brutes like Mic. His surrogate donors were counting down the days until they'd be free of him the same way I was.

"What's your favorite Petty song?" Natalie asked as I doctored her wrist afterward.

"Learning to Fly." *Story of my life*, I thought with a soft snort.

She leaned across the bed and clicked a button on her player until she found it. Then she lay back on the bedspread, her tangle of colorful hair splaying out in a halo around the one side of her head. She was wearing her ratty jean vest today, with a faded, Heartbreakers tour tee shirt underneath.

"Is that the real deal?" I asked, leaning back on one elbow.

She nodded. "From the eighties. One of my former patrons gave it to me."

I bristled at the thought of another vampire feeding on

Natalie, but I didn't say anything. *Stupid, useless emotions.* I felt ridiculous for having them. No one flipped out over their hairstylist having other clients, or their gynecologist seeing other patients. I wondered how long it would take before I stopped feeling like everyone I bit was *mine.*

Natalie and I lay on her bed, silently listening to the best of Tom while I played with her hair, separating and braiding each color. When it was time for me to leave for Kai's law class, she stood to give me a hug.

"Will you stop by to see me again after your feeding with Sampson later?" she asked.

"Sure." I squeezed her, breathing in the smell of her bubblegum-scented shampoo. *Two months.*

As I headed down the hallway, I wondered what the chances were of convincing her to go to college in St. Louis. I had a feeling she and Mandy would get along just fine. Though, Mandy probably wouldn't be thrilled about having to share a room again.

The daydream was farfetched, but it brought a smile to my lips.

Vampire law was every bit the snoozefest human law had been. The classroom consisted of two long, concrete tables with matching benches set before a smaller table that served as Kai's desk. He at least had a cushy-looking chair to sit in. The rest of us dealt with aching tailbones that persisted throughout combat training most days.

Today, we were covering the vampiric legal system. It was familiar content that dragged at my eyelids, especially as Kai's smooth, deep voice read from the course textbook.

"Like with human law, vampiric law works on the notion that one is innocent until proven guilty. But compared to the human court system, vampiric court is simple and concise. Punishments are more severe, but due to our extended lifespans, crime tends to be more severe, as well. Undead offenders are emboldened by their bloodlust. Which is why scion creation is so heavily regulated."

Mic snorted. "And why sireless vamplings are usually put down like stray dogs."

Kai glared at him even as he nodded. "If they are unregistered and have no one to attest to their endurance and discipline." His eyes were kinder when they found me. "Though the rare few who are pardoned often thrive and work vigilantly to overcome their handicap."

My face warmed at the insinuation that I was somehow less capable than the fashion police reject who hadn't matured past his days as a schoolyard bully.

Kai turned a page and went on. "Since many households

are run through trusts established via human channels and pay taxes as such, it is imperative that vampiric tax be kept as minimal as possible. Punishment methods for offenders are designed with this in mind. Sentencing costs undead taxpayers very little, and the public service rulings more than make up for the expense involved with the more severe verdicts of execution and, at the maximum extent of the law, coffin-locking."

"Wait." I didn't care how ignorant I would look to the others. I had to ask. "So it's public service, death, then coffin-locking? That's the order of severity?"

"Here we go." Blair huffed and tossed her fiery ponytail over her shoulder before glaring at me. "Don't worry, green fang. We all get to hang out in a coffin for three days before training is complete. You'll understand why then."

My jaw unhinged. *Three days?* I was expected to go three days without feeding?

Kai cleared his throat. "Let's move on. We have a lot more to cover."

I blinked around the room, seeing if anyone else was as alarmed by the news as I was. Emma frowned at me before turning her attention up to the front of the classroom. No one else seemed riled in the slightest. Had their sires prepared them for this? Had I somehow missed it in Roman's notes? Could I even consider doing something that dumb and dangerous?

Kai resumed the lesson despite my obvious distress. "The categories of crime addressed by vampiric law are divided into three categories: violation of the blood, violation of the peace, and violation of the house. These correlate closely with the three forms of punishment. Violations of the blood, which are most often accidental harem deaths at the hands of untrained vamplings, result in a public service sentencing where the vampling can be more closely supervised until their bloodlust is under control."

I remembered when Roman had caught up with me after I'd taken a bite out of a creep trying to carjack me in East St. Louis. He'd mentioned something about indentured servitude being a possible punishment—if he'd followed through and arrested me as he should have.

Kai continued. "Violations of the peace are more serious, though they can and do often overlap with blood violations. They occur when a vampire's actions risk exposing our kind to humans as a whole, even in an unintentional way. Posting a video of you feeding on social media, for instance, would most likely result in a death sentence."

"That seems a little extreme," I injected, finally coming out of my stupor at learning I'd soon be getting a three-day coffin nap. "People make mistakes. They're human."

"We *were* human," Blair said, giving me another of her

annoyed glares. "Now, we're vampires, and as such, we have a responsibility to keep the peace through secrecy."

"Yes." Kai nodded, pleased with her reply. "That's an excellent way to look at it. A human doing something ignorant for the world to see does not put their species in danger the same way a vampire's actions can. And, statistically speaking, when a punishment is more severe, the crime is less frequent."

The corners of my mouth sagged, but I didn't say anything more on the subject. Blair wasn't the only one shooting daggers at me now. If I couldn't keep quiet long enough for Kai to get through the lesson, we were going to end up running over. And then Sergeant Sorano would push us extra hard through combat training, possibly letting it eat into our second harem timeslot.

"Last one," Kai said. "Violations of the house. When a vampire's crime is against another vampire, namely against a noble or royal household. This crime is dealt the most severe punishment of being coffin-locked, a fate worse than death"—he raised both eyebrows at me, as if in challenge, but I didn't interrupt this time—"because it can last for decades, centuries even, if the crime is serious enough. These crimes range anywhere from a verbal insult at a house master to murder. The only way a vampire can escape a coffin-lock sentence is if the accuser challenges them to a blood duel—"

"They still do those?" Sonja interrupted this time, saving

me from having to myself. Of course, I would have rather she asked what the hell a blood duel was in the first place.

Kai grimaced and cocked his head. "They're rare these days, but the law remains on the books." When he noticed my confusion, he added, "Like a Wild West gun duel, blood duels are to the death. The challenger risks dying themselves, of course, but they also stand to gain a more immediate and permanent retribution for whatever slight they incurred."

"Who would be stupid enough to accept a challenge like that over facing a fair trial?" I asked.

Mic snorted. "You really don't know anything, do you? Blood duels can't be refused."

Kai gave me a grim nod.

"What kind of fucked up law is that?" I glared at both of them.

My outburst changed the atmosphere immediately. The fact that I had been human more recently than anyone else in the room—several *decades* more recently—was so painfully obvious. Mic's jab that I had no business training with seasoned scions came back to me, and heat boiled under my skin.

Kai closed the book on his desk and folded his arms on top of it. His dark eyes met mine with thoughtful consideration, if a little malice. "While I'd love to dissect every last law that you don't agree with, Ms. Skye, we simply don't have that kind of time to waste in my classroom. To help bring you up to speed, your harem time will be cut in half for the next week so you can lend a hand in the records department. Perhaps the history within those stacks will give you a better appreciation for the reasons behind our laws."

I broke eye contact with him and scowled at my desk, refusing to acknowledge Mic's and Blair's snarky chortling. The harem was the only thing I actually enjoyed about this godforsaken place.

There wasn't a chance in hell I'd open my mouth again in Kai's class. Not if that was the price.

Chapter Ten

Kai's sentence didn't begin until the next night when Alice would have an outlined task list for me. I was to meet her on the second floor of the library building, where the records department was located. She oversaw it in addition to the library.

After class, the cadets met up with Sergeant Sorano again. Combat training took an interesting turn when she passed around a box of silver-plated handcuffs. The metal burned when it touched my skin, and if I held on to it long enough, blisters formed. Roman's notes mentioned the silver affliction, but it still baffled me.

I wanted to know *why* silver was such a deal breaker, but I was sure that was another newbie question that would just result in additional taunting. So I filed it away to ask Sonja later and kept my mouth shut—except for occasionally cursing through my teeth—as we took turns wrestling each other to the ground and applying the cuffs. The pain was *almost* as bad as the time I had to take a shot of pepper spray to the face at the police academy.

Sorano informed us that we would have leather gloves for using the cuffs once we were agents, but it was vital that we have the endurance to work with them even if we didn't have time to slip on protection. I could barely grip the door handle to the harem afterward.

My feeding with Sampson healed most of the damage to my phalanges, and it also allowed me enough time to visit Natalie again, as I'd promised. The relief gave way to regret as I explained why she wouldn't be seeing as much of me over the next week.

"That's so unfair." She fumed as she undid the braids I'd put in her hair earlier and then did a double take when she caught her reflection in the mirror above her dresser. Her rainbow hair frizzed in all directions, the natural crimps giving it an Einstein-esque appearance that was only reinforced by the smooth span of scalp adjacent to it.

"Wowza." I mashed my lips together, trying to suppress the laughter cramping up my stomach.

Natalie glowered at me. "Yeah, let's not try that one again."

I held off asking her my vampy research questions and opted to scour the library, even though I'd be spending plenty of time there soon enough. The scholarly building was quickly becoming another safe place for me on base. Mic hadn't returned since Sonja sent him packing, and Alice even seemed to be warming up to me. I was hoping that meant she'd cut me some slack in records.

I had two things in particular that I wanted to look up tonight. The first was something I'd skimmed in one of the biology books written for human agents hoping to eventually become scions. Something about lifeblood, which I had assumed was what a vampire fed to a human in order to turn them. Roman had called it being anointed. But then a passage about the brink of death forging a blood bond akin to a consummated marriage ritual caught my attention. I was second-guessing everything now.

The other thing I wanted to know the answer to was a new question spurred by the *delightful* lesson in class tonight. It didn't take a rocket surgeon to figure out that the laws and punishments Kai covered were mostly meant for the middle-class vamps. Scarlett's and Raphael's exile was proof enough of that. But I was curious. What kind of crimes justified exiling a royal vampire? I started with that question, seeing as how it was the less embarrassing of the two.

Upon entering the library, I caught a glimpse of Alice as she disappeared up the stairs in the back corner. I wasn't sure if I should take her disappearing act as an insult or as her expressing that she trusted me alone in her domain. The few times I'd braved asking for her help to find something, she had complied, though my very human questions seemed to alarm her. I was glad for the privacy tonight.

I found the tome regarding royal vampire etiquette and customs hidden on a bottom shelf among a collection of dry, historical reads about vampire standings through various global and domestic wars. My eyes tended to glaze over when faced with books that surpassed a thousand pages, so I'd stuck to the briefer texts. I guessed it was time to expand my horizons.

The table of contents for this new book find was a chapter in itself, but it was a chapter worth reading. It took five false starts before I finally found the section I needed. It detailed how the structure of a royal family shifted and how assets were dispersed after a death. And it contained the only reference I'd found so far to an exiled royal.

The Prince of House Baumgartner, the vampire family that reigned in Austria, had murdered his sire, the king, in the seventeenth century. The prince had been coffin-locked—and unless vampires had some sort of appeals court, he was still there. The king's other scion, the princess, was promoted to queen. The prince's scion was offered the station of prince if he would swear fealty to the new queen and denounce his ties to his sire—a tall order for any scion. He refused, but since he had no knowledge of the prince's murderous plans, he was exiled instead of executed.

Exile for vamps was different than for humans. They weren't necessarily expected to flee the country, but they did have to relinquish all of their royal assets and staff, including their harem, who were considered employees of the house proper.

The prince's scion was tossed out on his ass to start over

from scratch. He was essentially homeless, having to find shelter and willing donors all over again. If he couldn't manage or violated any of the vampiric laws in the process—which would be easy to do in such a state of upheaval—then he would be brought up on charges of his own. It almost seemed like that was the end goal, a sharp jab in the wrong direction so the powers that be had better reason to slap him with the book and coffin-lock him in the basement alongside his sire.

I didn't care how unjust it was—I refused to feel sorry for Scarlett or Raphael. What they had done to me, to Will, to Mandy…it was unthinkable. I was relieved that Mandy had taken care of Raphael, and that there was no evidence of it after she'd made a quick meal of him.

The small bit of his blood that had made me into who—*what*—I now was held no sway over me. I didn't have some tender place in my heart for the bastard who'd killed my partner and then murdered me. If anything, I considered Mandy my maker. It'd been her sloppy feasting that had resulted in me rising to fight another night.

And maybe that was another reason I felt so compelled to keep the girl under my wing. Not that she actually needed the coddling. Mandy had grown up homeless on the streets of St. Louis. She'd been abducted, hooked on heroin, and turned into a werewolf before being forced to work in the Scarlett

Inn. But she'd escaped the vampire brothel and made her way to a rehab center for supernaturals, and then, she'd come back to help the other girls. I admired her. She deserved to have someone watching her back, someone willing to show her what the tail end of a normal childhood might have looked like if she'd been a more fortunate daughter.

My eyes glassed over as I skimmed the chapter. I had no interest in how the king's, the prince's, or the prince's scion's fine clothing or carriages were dispersed or auctioned off. So I skipped ahead to the next section, regarding what happened to their potential scions, the half-sired humans stuck in limbo after the whole catastrophe had gone down.

The prince's half-sired scion had slipped away in the night after the murder. Some suspected that he was an accomplice, but without another vampire to sustain him, his human age would result in his demise in a matter of months, a year at best. They hadn't bothered to hunt him down.

The king had had one half-sired scion, a woman who'd been with him for over two hundred years. She'd gone mad and killed herself. Once risen as a vampire, she took her un-dead life by greeting the sun that morning. Lifeblood was mentioned briefly, and I cringed, remembering I needed to look that up next.

I reshelved the book and began my hunt anew, reading each title as I prowled the stacks. So many of them caught my attention. It was a struggle not to lose sight of my quest. *The Art of Bloodletting. Harem Structure and Maintenance. The Freelance Donor. Rich Blood: Feeding Your Harem for Health and Prosperity.* I would have to make a point to ask Alice where I could get my hands on some of these books off base. They couldn't be the only copies available.

The next book I finally settled on wasn't anywhere near the texts about vampire biology and anatomy where I'd expected it to be. It was shelved with the leisure reads, tucked between a book about historical vampire power couples and a collection of love poems written by a vampire named Ambrogio to his lover Selene titled *The Blood Will Run.* Creepy stalker alert, anyone?

The less alarming title of the book I spread out on the table was *Blood Relations and Ceremonies.* It was a bit archaic, and I wasn't even sure if it was relevant to the modern vampire community anymore. Not with instructions on how to budget a dowry for a new scion that went so far as to suggest presenting them with their very own horse and carriage. A proper scion should not have to share a coach with their former harem companions, apparently. And potential scions were referred to as "human servants." At least the modern vamps had attempted to jump on the social justice wagon and replaced the crude term with the more acceptable "half-sired scion" or "potential scion." But the book did have a chapter about the chemical reactions associated with lifeblood, so I gave it a second chance.

Lifeblood…was not the same thing as being anointed. Oh, no, it couldn't have been that simple. Anointing a potential scion and half-siring them involved a vampire sharing a little sip of their blood once or twice a week to keep them young and resilient, eager to do their *master's* bidding. If they died, they would then rise as a vampire and be an official scion. Story over.

Lifeblood was something else entirely. When I'd nearly died from extreme road rash and Roman had fed me enough of his blood to bring me back from the brink of true death— that had been lifeblood. And then when he had almost died after being stabbed at Nigel's party, and I'd brought him back by opening my wrist—that had been lifeblood.

Lifeblood was the strongest bond that could be formed with a vampire. It even surpassed the one between scion and sire—though that bond was sometimes established between them before the scion's first rising. Since a sire could no longer feed from a scion after that, the lifeblood bond often faded, like Roman and I were waiting for it to do now, I supposed. But there was no indication of how long it could take for that to run its course.

It was the reason he'd heard my call when I was trapped in the sinking coffin. And it was the reason I could hear him in my mind, soothing my panic. Did he know? Had he kept this from me, hoping it would go away and we'd never have to speak of it? Was the ache in my chest every time I heard his voice or pictured his face just some juvenile vampling reaction? The vampire version of puppy love?

I blinked up from the pages, my breath slowly mounting as if I might hyperventilate. The aisle of books my table was situated in seemed to constrict around me, lengthening to abstract proportions. The pulse in my head sounded like thunder. I was going to be sick.

Then Sonja's head poked around the corner of the shelf. "There you are."

"Nothing! What? Hi," I said, slamming the book closed.

Sonja's keen eyes caught the title along the spine before I could cover it. "You know you're not supposed to anoint anyone without the royal blessing, right?" she asked, cautiously glancing over her shoulder to make sure Alice wasn't eavesdropping from her desk.

I shook my head. "It was an emergency—he was about to die. And I didn't know at the time, and his potential sire has anointed him plenty since then, so I'm good…right?"

"Well, this sounds promising." She dropped into the seat across from me and grinned as she leaned across the table, her brown eyes sparkling. "Tell me something juicy, and I'll answer whatever question is plaguing you—with a straight face," she added, seeing my hesitation.

"Is my ignorance that amusing?"

Sonja winced sympathetically. "I gotta tell you. It's a bit like watching a newborn kitten try to raise itself in the jungle."

I snorted at her. "Well, don't hold back. Tell me how you really feel."

"Hey, I could blow smoke up your ass all night, but it won't get you too far. Besides, you're doing better than anyone expected you would."

"Fine." Flattery for the win. I pursed my lips and narrowed my eyes at her before finally caving. "I think I might have accidentally forged a lifeblood union with Vanessa Sorano's potential scion."

Sonja sucked in a sharp breath. "Oooh, scandalous." She pressed her lips together and snickered. "And what's this big scary question you're hunting for the answer to?"

"How long before this wears off?" I begged. Wasn't that obvious? What the hell else would I need to know?

"Sweetie." Sonja gave me a comforting smile. "That's like asking how long love takes to wear off. Maybe tomorrow, maybe never. No one really knows." Panic fisted my guts, but Sonja reached across the table and patted my hand. "But he'll be fully turned eventually, and that tends to do the trick. Don't worry yourself sick over it. Just invest in an extra hunky harem donor or two."

"Oh, really? You think that will do the trick?" I glared at her. "I should just have some pie since I can't have the cake?"

"Your human is showing." She raised a judgy eyebrow. "Might wanna tuck that back in if you want to be taken seriously around here."

I covered my face with both hands. "It's just not… I can't look at humans the same way the rest of you do."

Sonja stood and rapped her knuckles against the tabletop as she left. "Give it time, baby fangs."

Chapter Eleven

Records detention duty proved neither easy nor educational. And Alice did not like me, I soon realized. So the vampling bias extended beyond competitive cadets. Super.

The librarian vamp at least didn't hurl snide insults nonstop. There was class and couth to her animosity. Her disapproval was revealed in the way she all but refused to acknowledge my presence. When I showed up at the library and asked what I should do, she silently handed me a typed list of precise instructions and then pointed to the stairs leading up to the records department.

I spent forty-five minutes after my first harem break and forty-five minutes before my second harem break upstairs at the library, sorting through undead private records and filing them into a new set of cabinets that had been brought in.

The cabinets were the first exciting delivery made since I arrived at the bat cave, and several mystery boxes had been stashed inside the drawers. Sorano ordered us to unload and move them into her office within the barracks. One box proved to be the silver handcuffs. I wondered what new horrors awaited in the other packages.

After being emptied, we helped move the cabinets to the library and upstairs, positioning them around the lofted space at Alice's discretion. And there they'd sat, for nearly a week, empty and waiting. Almost as if the BATC sergeants were just waiting for someone to step out of line so they could offer Alice the needed help free of charge. Like I said, they were an efficient bunch.

But, Alice really did need the help. The records department was like a legal document time capsule. Storing tax forms, birth certificates, scion appointments, living wills, and all those other miscellaneous things for vampires who were, in some cases, several hundred years old…well, it created a lot of paperwork. A lot of questions, too. Since we were working with some seriously sensitive information here, it was hardcopy only. No digital files to risk being hacked.

Someone had to sort all that shit and keep it organized. And when it outgrew its current filing system, someone had to transfer all that shit to its new home. That someone might as well be me. I was an easy target, after all.

My library research was put on hold that week, and I didn't even get an update on Mandy's trip until she'd been back for several days. We met outside the cafeteria at the picnic table again, along with Collins. He watched me the whole time Mandy relayed the details of the elk hunt through the mountains she'd participated in. How, after feasting on the thing's carcass, she'd slept in a dogpile with a dozen other wolves. How it was the most exhilarating and liberating night of her life, and she couldn't wait to go back. When she finally caught on to Collins' edgy vibe, her voice trailed off.

"What?" I barked at him. His eyeballing was creeping me out.

He frowned and bit the tip of his tongue as if trying to find the right words. "Why didn't you tell me you had a reputation with these people?"

"A reputation?" I scoffed. "Hilarious."

"Is it?" He clenched his teeth and blinked at me. "You mean you didn't help bring down a brothel run by the exiled Baroness of House Lilith?" He huffed at my guilty-as-sin expression. "Yeah, I know about that. And I know that you also shot and killed two former blood donors of that baroness. Oh, and one of the half-sired cadets is convinced that you're fucking the duke because no one as green as you has ever been accepted to train here before."

"Okay, okay." I held up a finger as his voice escalated. "Those first two, they were about confidential cases. I couldn't share the details with you, legally-speaking. And as for the duke, no! Of course not."

Collins threw out his hands, palms up. "Then how do you explain it?"

"I was only given an interview with him after I helped with that last case, and that was all dumb luck anyway," I said, pausing to marvel at how I could ever consider a serial killer breaking into my house lucky. "I begged to be allowed here—

I pleaded on your behalf, too. Remember? Both of you." My eyes flicked to Mandy. At least one person was grateful for that effort.

"The baroness is still at large." Collins blew out a heavy sigh and glanced around the base. His arms wrapped around his chest, and he rocked softly on the bench. "You are in real danger, Jenna. You know that, right?"

I tried to laugh it off, but hearing it summed up that way wasn't very inspiring. "I was a cop just as long as you were, Collins. I've had my fair share of death threats from people I've put away."

"But this one isn't put away," he hissed, leaning in closer to me as he whisper-shouted. "And she's a psychotic vampire who's already sent her harem after you once."

"And once we're on Blood Vice, I'm going to request to be put on her case," I said, daring him to challenge me. I was not some damsel prepared to run off and hide until the big boy vampires took care of the problem. Who knew how long that might take? And why should I wait around like a helpless sap anyway? I never would have before when I was a human officer. It just wasn't who I was.

Collins looked at me as if I'd gone mad. "What the hell have you gotten me into?"

I rolled my eyes. "What kind of bad guys did you *think* we'd be dealing with, Collins? Honestly?"

"Bad guys like the one you let get away at that DUI checkpoint! Yeah, don't think I didn't put two and two together after I found out about your…condition." He waved a hand at me.

We all fell quiet as another cadet walked past on their way to the phone booth. I hadn't used up my full allotment of time, but I couldn't bring myself to call Roman again, and Vin hadn't answered. I didn't bother leaving a message on his voicemail. I had a bad feeling that he didn't trust himself not to slip up and say something about his research that might result in me not coming home.

"I'm sorry," I finally said to Collins. "If I'd known it was hot gossip, I would have said screw the rules and told you about the cases myself. And if it's too much for you, I'll understand. I can even find a new donor to replace you if that's what you want. I have more connections now."

He swallowed and looked down at his boots. Clearly, I wasn't the only one dreaming up ways to walk away from this. We were four weeks in, with eight more to go. I didn't expect to reach a cracking point so soon. I thought again of Vanessa and the fifty years she'd spent doing this. Did Roman admire that about her?

"I'll stay for now," Collins said. "But I make no promises. I have a husband to think of, and I don't like the idea of putting him in danger over all this vampire Godfather bullshit."

"Fair enough." I sighed and reached out to squeeze his shoulder. "I mean it, though. No hard feelings if you change your mind. Same goes for you," I said, turning to Mandy.

She cracked a small grin. "Never thought I'd be the one in love with boot camp while you two fell apart. I'm almost sorry we're not staying longer. We only have two moon camps left. I may have to find a local chapter with Blood Vice and see where they meet up every month."

"Seriously, is there some rule that says you can't bite me?" Collins asked her. "I mean, she might be too far gone to be saved"—he jerked his head in my direction—"but I'd take being able to lick my own nuts over the nonsense I've been dealing with in a heartbeat."

Mandy and I groaned in unison.

"Boys are so gross." She shook her head.

Collins poked her in the ribs as he stood. "Says the butt sniffer who brags about eating raw guts and sleeping in dogpiles."

The days dragged on. Blair and Mic continued to taunt me, even though I'd stopped interrupting the law class. My library research resumed, and I shared another few illuminating conversations with Sonja.

My body also began to show real signs that the training was doing something. My muscles were hard as granite beneath my skin. My waist had narrowed, showing off the chords of muscles spanning above my hips, and I suddenly had abs. Where had those come from? My fatigue shirt also felt tighter across my shoulders and chest.

Near the end of week six, Sorano revealed the contents of another of the mystery boxes we'd stashed in her office.

"Most of you already have some experience with firearms, so we're going to skip over the beginner's course and move right in to intermediate," Sorano said, pacing before a table that held seven military rifles. "This is the Moba M4 semi-automatic, Blood Vice's custom raid firearm. Once you're assigned to a field office, you will be issued one of these along with the standard sidearms." She paused to pick one up and ejected the magazine. "Each of these holds thirty rounds of SW 5.56, but we'll be working with Peart marking rounds through training."

I'd never heard of the rifle model or ammunitions before, but I was guessing the SW stood for Silver Wolfsbane. The practice rounds were likely a product of Sorano Munitions, too.

"We'll be spending today's and tomorrow's sessions in the tunnel range. Once you've each passed the easy marksman test, we'll move on to the tactical applications course. Three buildings in the southwest corner of the base have been staged to simulate real-world raid scenarios. Master all three, and you'll earn your first night off. A limo will take you into Denver Saturday evening and return you to base early Sunday morning." Sorano's glare sharpened. "Unless you come in last place. Then you'll be spending Saturday night at the library, assisting Alice with the records transition. I'm sure Skye can confirm how stimulating that work is."

I cringed at the jab but kept my mouth shut. That had been a difficult lesson to learn, but a valuable one among the bloodsucking elite. I now knew to save my energy because each day proved how badly I would need it.

The tunnel range was just that—a range inside a tunnel. It opened off the southern perimeter of the base and stretched almost twice the distance that I'd had to test out with a rifle to earn my certification at the police academy. The service rifle I'd been issued from my previous precinct had never left the trunk of my patrol car.

I'd known there would be rifle training at some point, considering the firearms I'd seen Roman and Vanessa's unit toting around at the barn raid and during the undercover sting at Bleeders. There just hadn't been enough time to brush up on that particular skill before my sentence at the bat cave began. And finding a range that was open during my waking hours was no piece of cake either.

I was rusty, but I had this crazy idea that maybe it would be like riding a bike, especially now that I was a vampire. Of course, I'd also had the naivety to think that I'd be granted fancy vampy superpowers at first, too. But there'd been no welcome party bearing a velvet cape. No eagle-eye vision improvement or hypnotic abilities. Sure, I had the creepy blood vision—the *Eye of Blood,* as Roman had called it—that served as little more than a mood ring or one of those fancy lights that revealed invisible ink. I might as well have gotten it out of a cereal box.

Like with everything except the cave pool, I came in last. But, by the end of the session, I was at least improving. I just had to focus on competing with myself and not the others. If we'd been working with handguns, I would have given these arrogant vamps a run for their money.

The second session was even better—though, I was still the weakest link. There was no denying that. I was not ready for the raid scenarios, but Sorano would not be delaying the training schedule so the *duke's pet vampling* could keep up. I hadn't wanted to believe Collins when he shared the rumor, but overhearing Blair in the showers was all the confirmation I needed.

Early Saturday morning, we stood before Sergeant Sorano in full gear, the Moba M4s angled across our chests.

"In and out," Sorano barked. "You'll do this in pairs, each time with a new partner. Whatever squabbles you have with each other, put them on hold. Right now, you're professionals doing a job. Act like it."

Everything was set up to work in tight rotation. We were playing musical raids. For the first exercise, I was paired with Andre Freeman. The tall, dark, and annoyed vamp grimaced when he heard my name announced alongside his, but he nodded his acceptance without complaining.

"I'll go in first and clear the upstairs. You take the rooms on the main level. We'll finish faster that way," he said as we each loaded a magazine of marker rounds laid out for us on a table.

I nodded without looking at him. "Yeah, sure."

We were being timed on top of being evaluated for accuracy and efficiency. Someone would be watching us on each level, rewarding points for good work and docking points if we screwed up. I was already sweating under my fatigues, my nerves twitching anxiously.

The scenario Andre and I were walking into was a rogue nest raid. Sometimes, as I learned in Kai's class, a vampire decided that they were above the law, and they went all willy-nilly with the siring, creating their own vampling army and plotting to overthrow House Lilith. As if.

Blood Vice was often tasked with dismantling these

setups. Baby scions were given the opportunity to turn themselves in for judgment from the high council—which frequently resulted in execution but, occasionally, saw them adopted by other vamps. If they resisted arrest, the Blood Vice agents were to fire at will. The use of deadly force wasn't a hot-button issue in the supernatural community the way it was for humans. Threats were black and white when dealing with our kind. A lengthy standoff meant more human casualties and risk of exposure because human police response time was far superior to what it had been before the invention of the automobile.

Andre and I took our places behind the white line that separated the cadets from the training buildings. The others were preparing to enter their own scenarios, Sonja and Emma at the second building, and Blair and Mic at the third. In our black fatigues, our rifles at the ready, we looked like we could actually be a legitimate and foreboding unit. The buzzer sounded, and we moved.

I flanked the exterior door and waited for Andre to kick it in. Then I followed him inside the building. It was dark, but I heard the hiss of voices all around us. As my eyes adjusted, my blood vision tinged the room in a soft shade of dusty red. I picked out Sergeant Carmichael in the corner, a clipboard tucked in the crook of her arm. She wore a pair of night vision goggles strapped to her head.

Andre's elbow bumped my shoulder. "You got this?" he whispered, nodding toward the stairs he intended to take. I nodded back.

"Go."

I headed for the first room on the lower level. Several mattresses were strewn around the floor, but I didn't see any bodies. No vampires cutting across the blood haze in living color.

My fingers gripped my rifle tighter as I reached the door to the second room. I took a deep breath and shoved it open. A vampire in the corner greeted me with a savage hiss. I aimed, but I held steady. *Don't be impulsive, Jenna.*

"Stand down," I shouted. "Stand down!"

She held her hands up and dropped to her knees. The tip of my rifle dipped, but then movement caught the corner of my eye. I turned and aimed again, ready to fire, but my breath rushed out instead.

Mandy stood in the room, her hands lifted, fingers curled comically like a horror film monster. She made to jump at me again, her eyes bulging with unspoken frustration, and I realized I was expected to shoot her. I did, but it came too late. The marker round grazed her shoulder as I was pushed to the floor by the vamp I'd first encountered.

I rolled and used the shoulder stock of my rifle to push the woman off me, quickly twisting the firearm around to blast her in the stomach and chest with four shots. One missed her entirely and struck the ceiling of the room.

The vampire grunted as the marker rounds made impact. At this range, the practice ammunition was plenty uncomfortable. She glared at me, but she dropped to her knees again. Her eyes darted to Mandy, who remained standing against the wall, the thin spatter of paint on her arm not nearly enough to take down a human, let alone a vamp or werewolf.

"What the hell are you waiting for?" the vampire snapped at her.

I didn't give Mandy a chance to answer. I tagged her in the chest with a single round and hurried out of the room. Andre was waiting near the front door. His eyes narrowed when he spotted me.

"Come on," he hissed.

We were the last team to finish. And Mandy's hesitation had not gone unnoticed. She'd taken it easy on me. I'd been surprised to see her, but to be fair, raids were full of surprises. Carmichael docked a hefty number of points for the blunder.

I was relieved to hear Sonja's name called out with mine when Sorano paired us up for the second scenario. Sonja looked less thrilled about the union, but she gave me a tight smile as we met up at the ammunition table before the building and loaded fresh magazines.

"I've been watching you at the range," she said under her

breath. "You need to keep both eyes open and get your rifle stock off your arm and into your shoulder."

"You couldn't have said something sooner?" I made a face at her, but she only shrugged.

"Didn't know I'd be relying on you in order to score a night out on the town."

I harrumphed and readjusted the stock of my rifle against my shoulder as we lined up.

The buzzer sounded again. I quickened my step this time, rushing up to the building as fast as my legs would carry me.

The second scenario was a rescue mission. We had to work together to separate the vampire from their victim. The vampire, depending on their household's status, and the status of the household their victim had been taken from, would either be executed or coffin-locked. So it was preferable that they be brought in rather than killed on the spot. Any scions, half-sired scions, or harem donors who resisted were fair game.

We were working with the silver cuffs again. Without gloves. Though, the stand-in vampire villains were given protection. Sonja and I found them on the second floor after swiftly clearing the first. There were three of them, standing over an altar covered in...real blood?

The smell of it tickled my nose, and I heard Sonja's sharp intake of breath, too. The human strapped to the altar, playing victim, was Collins. I was less surprised this time, now that I was looking for him.

"Stand down!" Sonja shouted at the vamp standing behind the altar, his head dipped over Collins' throat.

Mine. Something triggered reflexively in my brain, and I stepped forward. If that vampire got any closer to my donor, I'd unload every last practice round into his face. And then I'd beat him to death with the stock.

Something flashed in the corner of my eye, and I jerked, turning to find another vampire charging at Sonja. My hyper-stimulated nerves were full of wrath, and I fired before I could think twice about it.

Sonja fired next, taking out a human playing half-sired underling. "Stand down!" she shouted at the master vamp again.

We circled the altar and each took him by an arm, stepping down on his calves as he dropped to the floor. Sonja gripped the back of his neck as I cuffed his wrists, not even feeling the sting of the silver. I was still too amped.

I leaned over Collins and touched his cheek, tilting his head aside to look at the fake wounds spanning his neck and chest. "Are you okay?"

"Just makeup," he whispered. "They're timing you. Get out of here."

Sonja yanked our faux perp up and led him downstairs,

giving me a sympathetic frown over her shoulder. After we'd turned him in to the sergeant waiting outside, she squeezed my arm.

"That was a cheap shot, but you impressed me, baby fangs."

Mic and Emma spilled out of the first house a second later. They both scowled at us. I smiled back, feeling smug that I hadn't come in last this time. Until Sorano announced that Blair would be my partner for the third and final scenario.

This should go well.

Chapter Twelve

I didn't think the last raid scenario would be so difficult. I was out of harem donors for the sergeants to surprise me with. What more could they spring on me?

"This one is a royal raid," Sorano explained.

My heart leapt into my throat, and I thought I might choke on it as I tried to suck in my next breath. They were fucking with me. There was no other explanation for it. God, did everyone want to see me fail so badly?

"This nest is heavily guarded," Sorano went on. "We've included moving targets to supplement the live ones for extra marksmanship points. You're allowed to shoot at everything except the royal target." She held up a picture of the male werewolf from Mandy's unit. "You'll be using marker rounds with a different color of paint this time, to distinguish your shots from everyone else's for accurate scoring." She nodded at the table behind us.

As the sergeant moved on to the next pair of cadets, Blair's menacing face angled toward me, the corners of her pale lips peeling back to expose clenched teeth. "Don't you dare fuck this up for me, green fang. My sire is delivering my personal harem to the city tonight, and I mean to enjoy them."

I gave her a contemptuous smile and retreated to the table, ignoring her as I grabbed a magazine and inserted it into my rifle. Talking to these hoity-toity vampires never accomplished anything worthwhile. I was just glad they were intended for field offices far, far away from St. Louis. The closest one I could even begin to worry about bumping into was Sonja, with her family home being in Ann Arbor, Michigan. I could live with seeing her again.

We lined up and waited for the buzzer. My ears pricked at the hum of the overhead lights far above us. At the sound of my breath as I tried to steady it. At the scratch of Sorano's pen on her clipboard. I watched as she lifted her hand, signaling whoever manned the buzzer. And then we were off.

The door to the third building smacked the interior wall as Blair and I both kicked it. Her eyes narrowed, but she kept them trained ahead along with the barrel of her rifle. The artificial light from outside spilled around us and through the open door, illuminating dust particles and reaching into the shadows of the structure.

Noise from the other two raids filtered in behind us. Gunshots and shouts to stand down. Our scenario was disturbingly quiet by comparison.

A stairwell divided the lower level. As we split up to circle it, a moving target that looked like a snarling wolf dropped from the ceiling, and I tagged it in the snout. I considered firing a second round, but I only had thirty to work with, and another target was fast approaching.

This one was live—one of the half-sireds from the human unit. Collins had pointed him out as one of the assfaces he thought needed their own unit. I spared two extra rounds for him, considering the sacrifice worth it until three moving targets on rails sped across the room toward me.

I jumped out of the way and riddled the plastic vamps with paint, but my pride fell flat as I realized there was still a second floor to raid, and I was down to a dozen rounds at best. Less than ten, after taking out another wolf target behind the stairwell.

Blair met me at the mouth of the stairs. "Quit being wasteful. You only have eight shots left," she grumbled as she whipped her red braid over her shoulder. I was mortified that she'd been counting my shots as well as her own, and also mildly alarmed. *Eight shots? Really?*

I followed Blair upstairs, letting her take out the first two targets. We still hadn't caught a glimpse of our royal mark. I had a bad feeling we would both be out of ammo before that happened.

When we reached the second level, we were swallowed by darkness. I clicked on the tactical light attached to the pic rails of my rifle. Blair did the same, and then she pointed two fingers to her left before heading off in the other direction.

The noisy racket of moving rails made the place sound like a carnival, but a youthful giggle quickly turned it into a house of horrors. I thought of Scarlett, and my skin crawled. A deep, bellowing Count Dracula laugh sent a chill up my spine, but then I quickly dismissed the extra noises as a recording of some sort. I needed to focus.

Blair's rifle fired from somewhere on the opposite side of the room. My blood vision flickered, and I made out a wooden box in the corner, likely housing a target. I inched closer, and sure enough, the thing flew open. A plastic Elvis bobbed forward as if he'd been spring-loaded. The hunk of burning love had seen better days. Paint splattered him head-to-toe. I had the foresight to be conservative and put a single round between his eyes.

The next target threw me off guard, hurtling through the open doorway of a hidden room. Cain Davis, the half-sired from House Hanson, tackled me to the ground and tried to wrench my rifle out of my hands.

My blood vision flared, turning his pale eyes and even paler hair bright red. He looked like an angel of death come to finish me off. I screamed in his face and managed to wedge a knee between him and the stock of my rifle. When that failed to offer enough leverage, I slammed my forehead into his chin.

He grunted and rocked back, reaching to touch his busted lip. The distraction opened a wider gap, so I planted a boot on his stomach and kicked hard, twisting the rifle away from him at the same time. I fired six rounds into his chest, leaving him in a graceless heap near Elvis.

I didn't care if it was a part of the exercise, the skirmish had shaken me. And now I was down to one round, with no royal vamp in sight. I stood and bolted for the stairwell, wondering why I couldn't hear Blair any longer.

I found her on the main level.

"Did you find him?" she asked, still scouring the room.

I frowned and shook my head.

"Fucking perfect." She sighed and pushed past me, heading back toward the stairs. "I've already double-checked your area down here. Might as well check upstairs, too." I'd had about enough of her patronizing trash talk.

"Watch out for your albino pet. He's quite the handful," I said, mirroring her snide face. "Maybe you should give him a little sip while you're up there, you know, before he goes full-on ghost."

Blair's fangs popped out, and she hissed at me. So melodramatic. "Cain is not *mine*."

The blood vision had worn off, so I had the pleasure of watching her pupils dilate until they ate away the green of her irises, and she looked like the wretched animal I knew her to be on the inside.

She slunk toward me, stalking like a jungle cat, forgetting the stairs and our mission. The end of her rifle lifted at the same time mine did. The difference was that mine was trained on the target trying to slip out the front door behind her.

Blair blinked, probably realizing my aim wasn't *that* bad, and twisted to look over her shoulder. "Don't!" she shouted, reaching for my rifle as I squeezed the trigger. "That's the royal!"

The target ducked and rolled out through the doorway just as my last round hit the backside of the metal door. It left a heavy indentation, almost going all the way through. No paint in sight.

Blair's eyes were still dilated when she turned around and emptied the rest of her marker rounds into my chest.

"Where the hell did you get a live round, Skye?" Sorano yelled in my face.

"I didn't know it was in the magazine, ma'am," I answered truthfully.

Blair snorted. She stood to my right, several yards away. It had taken Sorano and Kai both to pull her off me. The front of my fatigues was covered in purple paint, and I could feel the bruise forming over my breastbone. Another one ached around my eye socket, and a third lit up my jaw.

"Who's had access to your office?" Kai asked Sorano.

The sergeant opened her mouth to answer, but Blair huffed out an affronted sigh.

"You don't actually believe her?" She looked ready to claw my eyes out. "She could have killed that human. She could have killed *me*." Her eyes widened, and her fangs elongated again as if she had no control over them.

"Hanson!" Sergeant Sorano barked. "One more word, and you'll be staying behind with her tonight."

I winced at the results I'd been dreading ever since we were hauled from the building. The other four cadets had already headed for the barracks' harem to celebrate. And, of course, Blair wouldn't be forced to stay on base. Her sire was making a special trip. I didn't know why I'd even bothered to hope that the sergeant might cut me some slack.

That I'd almost shot the royal mark with a live round was terrible, no doubt about it. But that hadn't been my fault. And no one had even mentioned the dozen marker rounds Blair had unloaded on me. Were they blind? Was murdering your partner really preferable to killing a villain—a villain whom we'd likely have *orders* to put down if they weren't so fancy and privileged?

Blair swallowed her rage and inhaled in a deep, calming breath. She stared placidly at the sergeant, her gaze going vacant and still as death. I don't know what yogi had taught her that zen shit, but I wanted to meet them and know where they'd been all my life. The ability to shut off emotions as if they were on tap sounded handy as hell.

Sorano didn't find the trick quite so impressive. "You're dismissed, Hanson. Head back to the barracks."

"Yes, ma'am," Blair answered evenly. She left without sparing me another glance, not even a sideways one as she walked past me. I waited until she was a good distance away before pleading my case.

"I swear, I didn't know there was a live round in there. It was laid out on the table for me. When would I have found time to empty the entire magazine, load a live round, and then reload the thing? It could have just as easily been picked up by Blair."

Sorano threw her hand up, silencing me. "Either way, cadet, you came in last for the first scenario, and then bombed the third one. Report to Alice as soon as you rise tonight."

"Yes, ma'am," I said, biting back any future protest. That would only result in more grunt work being piled on top of the miserable evening I'd be spending by myself.

I wanted to know who had put a live round inside that magazine. Had the practice ammunition been loaded before being delivered with the filing cabinets? Or had someone tampered with it in Sorano's office? I tried to remember who had set the magazines out for us in between scenarios, but I drew a blank.

I didn't even know if it had been intended for me or someone else. Was it a fluke? A random jerk move by some disgruntled employee between here and the factory? I wanted to know. But I'd been dismissed. The mystery wasn't mine to solve.

I sulked back to the barracks, dragging my feet even more when I remembered that my last harem visit before sunrise was with Ned.

Chapter Thirteen

I didn't linger in the crypt on Saturday night. As the others dressed in their civilian clothes, grinning like cats who knew they'd soon be eating canary, I yanked on my fatigue pants and tank top. Then I stuffed my feet down into my boots, not bothering with the laces until I was outside the barracks.

Mandy and Collins greeted me. The tracking watches they'd been issued were missing, leaving faint indentations on their wrists. They were wearing outfits they'd packed, too. Collins fussed with a button on his blue dress shirt, while Mandy knotted and unknotted the corner of her favorite Metallica tee shirt. They were having a hard time getting reacquainted with clothing other than the stiff, black fatigues we'd been wearing for six weeks straight.

"We passed the course." The strain in Collins' sympathetic smile made me want to puke. Mandy elbowed him in the ribs.

"But we can stay and offer a hand in the library, if you want," she said. Collins glared at her, but he nodded grimly.

"No, it's fine. You guys earned a night off." I sighed. "Besides, I could use the extra time for my research."

"How's that going, by the way?" Collins asked.

I thought of the lifeblood discovery and swallowed. "It's been…informative."

Mandy glanced over her shoulder to where the other wolf and human cadets were congregating around Kai's golf cart and two more. The meaty vamp professor looked more like the version I'd first met at Nigel's party, wearing a satiny, blue suit. He intended to have a night off as well, I guessed.

Sergeant Carmichael sat in the driver's seat of one of the carts beside Kai's, her foot propped up on the dash. I was a little shocked at her civilian clothes—jeans and a flannel shirt with the sleeves rolled up to her elbows. She spotted me through the living wall that Mandy and Collins had erected in their effort to hide me.

"Don't you have somewhere to be, Skye?" Carmichael shouted.

"Yes, ma'am." I nodded to my harem. "Be safe, and have fun." Then I stalked off toward the library across base.

The cave pool was quiet, and so was the obstacle course. The overhead lights through the inactive sections of the base had been dimmed, likely to conserve electricity. The artificial twilight seemed to amplify the echo of my boots on the concrete paths cutting through the bat cave. I quickened my pace but refrained from breaking into a jog.

I met Alice on the first level of the library. Though the snooty vamp wasn't my favorite person ever, I was somewhat disappointed to find her preparing to leave. Even as the base librarian, she'd worn the same fatigues as the rest of the non-harem staff. Tonight, she was in a ruffled, blue cocktail dress. It matched Kai's suit, and I wondered if the two of them had color-coordinated for some party they planned to attend together.

"The harem will remain on base, so you may take your regularly scheduled meal breaks. You know how the new filing system works, so I expect to see some quality progress when I return. Through the Ns, at the very least." It was the most she'd ever said to me at one time.

I blinked at her in surprise a moment before hastily answering. "Yes, ma'am."

She nodded once and then left, clicking off the majority of the downstairs lights and leaving a fresh silence to settle around me. The shadowy quiet was less ominous inside the library, though it stirred the questions scratching at the back of my mind.

The labyrinthine stacks between these walls had become my sanctuary. Over the past few weeks, I'd looked forward to searching through them nearly as much as I looked forward to my harem visits. These tomes spilled the secrets I was sure a proper sire would have revealed to me over time. The nostalgia of the undead authors when they spoke of their makers left an aching hole in my heart. I'd been thrust into this world, this culture, against my will. Yet I pined for the milestones I'd never cross, the nurturing I'd never experience.

I reined in my eagerness and made my way upstairs to the records. If I worked quickly, I might have a fair amount of time left over to read more about the vampire-werewolf alliance formed in the sixteen hundreds. I wondered if any of Mandy's studies were covering it. What pomp and circumstance had she missed out on through her own violent and unexpected introduction to this strange underworld?

My mind sharpened to a fine focus as I shuffled stacks of files into the new cabinets. The old cabinets had been emptied before being relocated to some other building on base, and the mountain of boxes crowded in the center of the room. I moved them like a busy ant, to and fro, until I'd broken into a light sweat.

I stayed at it for four hours. When I finally paused to count the empty boxes I'd cleared, I decided to allow myself a small reading break before my visit to the harem. I'd already reached the first of the *L*s, so it was looking hopeful that I'd have my work done in plenty of time.

I snuck downstairs and peeked around one of the stacks that boxed in Alice's desk. It was empty. Coast clear, I made for the corner containing the older, more fragile texts. Alice watched me carefully on the days I migrated to this section of the library.

The history book on American supernatural conflicts through the centuries was kept in a silver box screwed to the top of a low shelf. A sheet of museum glass revealed the treasure within. Two holes, large enough for a pair of hands to slip through, were carved into the bottom silver panel. I slipped on a pair of long, cotton gloves and held my breath as I reached inside to open the tome.

The werewolves had a longer history in America than the vampires. There was mention of other shapeshifters, too, but I focused on the wolfy bits, hoping to find some scrap of information that might prove useful for Mandy or the dynamic of our relationship.

I read for an hour, about uneasy truces and peculiar gift exchanges. Some of the packs seceded from the initial alliance and moved to more isolated areas where they could live away from the vampires, but some formed precarious relations with the vamps, going so far as to offer harem donors to certain households as a means of securing trust and partnership. At least there was no mention of them turning or offering up wolves as unwilling sex slaves, so there was that, I guessed.

When I'd exhausted my interest in supernatural-interspecies affairs, another silver-boxed book caught my attention. This one was untitled, and at the far end of the prestigious lineup. The last time I'd taken an interest in the row of captive writings, Alice's agitation had seemed to elevate the closer I moved to this one, but without her scowling gaze to warn me off, I could read in peace.

The book was old, but it had been well cared for, and though it lacked a title, there was an intricate design tooled into the cover. The crowned skull with fangs was unnerving, even framed by lilies and apple tree boughs. It leered up at me from the dark, oily leather, daring me to have a look inside. Something tugged at my consciousness as I opened the cover.

The pages within, while yellow with age, were coated with a clear substance that preserved their integrity. They felt stiff between my gloved fingers and hissed softly as I turned them. After bypassing a few blank pages, I found a family tree. The names were written in frilly calligraphy, and the haunting, dark imagery that bordered the page was drawn in black, red, and silver ink. The attention to detail was incredible. Glossy apples peeked through a canopy of leaves suspended over the list of names, and red blood oozed between the tree bark running down either side of the page where it dripped onto a pile of fanged skulls.

The royal family of House Lilith was not as vast as I'd imagined it to be, though it stretched back several centuries. Vampires were immortal, and their household names were only carried on through blood scions. Once I shed my human ignorance, it was obvious why their small families grew so slowly.

There were over seven billion humans on this planet. I'd fed on four of them this week alone. But every human turned was one more mouth to feed, one more vampling to educate and tame. And one less vein to tap. There was a balance that had to be maintained. I imagined that was why contracts like Roman's were such a common practice within Blood Vice.

At the top of the family tree was the name *Lilith*. At first, I disregarded it, deciding it was merely there to announce the family name. But when I looked closer, I noted an additional line of fine print under the branch the artful letters rested atop.

Her Majesty, the Queen of House Lilith, Mother of Eternal Blood. Laid to her forever rest, June 1st, 1785.

Like with everything new I learned lately, I was left with more questions than answers. What the hell was a forever rest? Was that some fancy way of saying she'd died?

The next branch contained three names: *Adam, Gabriella,* and *Lili.* They were familiar. I'd noticed them peppered throughout some of the older texts. Like Lilith, the fine print under Adam's name read that he'd been laid to his forever rest on the same day. He was also labeled as a prince, and the date of his "first rising" in the late fourteen hundreds was included. The black ink of Gabriella's name was traced with a thick outline of red. Her second line of information solved half the riddle of Lilith and Adam.

Her Highness, the Princess of House Lilith, first risen December 3rd, 1506. Slain in battle, September 5th, 1781.

So maybe a forever rest wasn't death? My mind regurgitated what it could of my high school history lessons. That would have been during the American Revolution. Had vampires fought for or against the British? Or had they played Switzerland and remained in the shadows?

I suddenly wished Kai's law class included more history. Like I needed something else to study. I mentally added the questions to my running list of things to research in my scarce free time and moved on. There were still a lot of pages left, so maybe I was just getting ahead of myself.

Under Lili's name were two lines of extra information.

Her Highness, the Princess of House Lilith, first risen October 1st, 1611.

Her Majesty, the Queen of House Lilith, ascended June 1st, 1785.

Had Lili laid Lilith and Adam to their forever rests? Maybe it *was* death, but worded nicer since the new queen was at fault? Was she an evil monarch who had taken over by force? Or had Lilith been a royal bitch, and Lili saved everyone by putting her and this Adam down for a long dirt nap? God, I had *so* many questions. It was driving me mad.

A string of silver ivy dripping with blood reached down from Lili's branch to the next row of names. There were just two this time. *Morgan* and *Alexander.* Both had risen in the early seventeen hundreds. They were listed first as duke and duchess, and then later as prince and princess. Morgan's name was stained with red ink like Gabriella's, but the explanation given for her demise was more vague, simply stating that she'd been *slain*. Twenty years ago.

Beneath Morgan's branch was one for a duchess named Ursula. Where had I heard that name before? My mind drew a blank as I took in the two remaining lines, naming Raphael and Scarlett as Ursula's scions. The exiled baron and baroness, though that detail had been left off their supplementary information. Either the book hadn't been updated, or the family didn't like to record and air any more dirty laundry than they had to.

A narrow bit of space remained along the bottom edge of the page. I imagined my name there and what it might say. What my title would be. What my demise would be recorded as. Then I wondered if I'd be recorded at all, or just swept under the rug of House Lilith's illicit history.

A shiver rocked my shoulders, and I turned my attention to the other side of the page where I'd left off with Prince Alexander. Beneath him, the name *Dante* caught my attention.

His Grace, the Duke of House Lilith, first risen May 7th, 1865.

Duke Dante. It had a nice ring to it. Though that baby face certainly hadn't looked like it was a hundred and fifty plus years old.

One other scion was listed for Alexander. Her frilly name read *Kassandra*, risen fifty years after Dante. Neither had scions of their own listed yet, but from the pattern I'd discerned, it was only a matter of time.

I wondered if they had any half-sired scions, or if any of them had ever gone through training at the bat cave. *Not likely.* I snorted. Then I thought of Cain Davis, and Blair's admission that he wasn't *hers*. Then just who the hell did he belong to? The sire of House Hanson maybe? Or another of Blair's sibling scions?

I abandoned the book and hurried back upstairs, trying to decide if I should begin my hunt in the *D*s or the *H*s. I decided to trace the paper trail back from Blair's file. Somewhere between her last fifty tax returns and the application for her most recent human documents, I found a copy of her scion appointment certificate. It was dated 1983.

Blair's sire was not Lord Hanson himself, but rather a scion of a scion of his. I jumped from file to file, searching for any hint of the white-haired underling's name. But before I found him, another name crossed my path. *Scarlett Lilosa.*

My fingers clenched the typed page, and I blinked several times, trying to clear my eyes. Hands shaking, I squatted to the floor and pressed my back against the cold filing cabinet. I took a deep breath and started reading from the top of the page again.

The official letterhead bore an insignia that resembled a simplified version of the crowned vampire skull I'd seen on the cover of the royal family's history book. It looked like a photocopy of a letter that must have been sent to House Hanson.

Official transfer order from the House of Lilith regarding the estate of Scarlett Lilosa.

The letter went on to detail the estate items Lord Hanson had won in the auction, and when he could expect them to be delivered. After a lengthy list of designer dresses crafted by none other than Wilhelmina Novak, the master sire of House Novak, and a collection of vintage Japanese war fans, I found the name I'd originally been looking for.

He was listed alongside several others, each noted for the service they had formerly provided Scarlett. A gardener, a chaperone, and her harem supervisor—C. Davis. Well. This was…*awkward.* With the rumors circulating around base, I had to imagine he knew of my run-in with his former master. I didn't know if the revelation should alarm me. With twenty years and a new household, how likely was it that he would care anyway?

I put the files back and decided to think on it more after my visit with Natalie. On my way downstairs, I stole another glance at Alice's desk. I was still alone.

The darkness seeping from the unlit corners of the library seemed to whisper out to me, beckoning me to peel back another layer of the mystery I'd become to myself. I wanted to stay longer and read beyond House Lilith's family tree. Whether they knew it or not, I was one of them now.

I shrugged off the impulse to trace my steps back to the guarded family tome and slipped down the aisle of leisure books. In the thin light, I struggled to read the titles as I fingered the shelf where I'd found the creepy love poems. Natalie would enjoy them, being the cheerful, bubblegum goth that she was.

As I pulled the volume free, a silhouette caught the corner of my eye. I yelped and dropped the book of poems before making out Sonja's springy curls. I hadn't heard her come in while I was upstairs.

"You scared the hell right out of me." I laughed as I bent down to fetch the book. "I thought you'd be out stalking the night with the others."

When Sonja didn't reply, I stepped closer, squinting through the darkness. A sole pendant lamp near the door spilled just enough light over the shelves and against her back that I could make out her shape and no more. Something in the perfect silence sparked my blood vision, causing the shadows to yield to the luminosity of my clandestine birthright.

Sonja's wrists were cuffed to the arms of the chair. Her blistered skin bubbled under the silver, but the casual drape of her fingers told me she couldn't feel the burn. Not anymore, at least.

The gaping hole in her chest, where her heart should have been, made sure of that.

Chapter Fourteen

An office existed on base for the rare few times a royal representative stopped in to check how the programs were going and to get an update for the duke. I'd asked Natalie at one point if the duke had ever visited himself. She'd told me that he hadn't in the two years she'd been there.

Aren't I special? I thought, as I sat in the royal office. The duke watched me from across the room, stealing glances in between reading from a file with my name on it. He'd asked Sergeant Sorano to leave the room, and for the first time, I thought she actually looked sorry for me.

"*¿Quién es tu creador?*" he asked again.

I licked my lips. "Pablo Zajalvo."

The duke, Dante, as I now knew, tilted his head to one side and gave me a lazy, friendly smile. His soft curls enhanced the flirty frat boy look he possessed. They disarmed me, and I found myself forgetting that he was an ancient, royal nobleman.

"I don't think you did this," he said, trying to put me at ease. My fingers clenched around the arms of the chair, and my knees bobbed with the adrenaline still rushing through my veins.

After discovering Sonja in the library and having a good old-fashioned panic attack, I went straight to the harem and found Marco, Mr. Blueblood. He'd known how to reach Kai in an emergency.

The sergeants all returned to base right away, discovering that the tunnel guard had been killed too, and the security feed tampered with. That was when the duke had been contacted. As devastating as circumstances were, everyone was shocked when he arrived to launch the investigation himself, along with a half-dozen personal guards, three hours before sunrise.

Dante watched me carefully, even as he explained his conclusion. "For one, you were the only cadet still wearing a training watch, and your vitals report shows no activity that could account for a struggle during the timeframe the coroner suggests that Sonja died."

"I *liked* Sonja," I said, struggling to make eye contact with him. I folded my hands together in front of my face and sighed. "She was the only cadet who was actually nice to me."

"Really?" He didn't sound surprised. "Why do you think that is?"

I shook my head. "I don't know. Maybe she felt sorry for me. Or maybe—"

"No." His eyebrows dipped up, giving him a deceptive air of sympathy. "Why do you suppose the others *aren't* nice to you?"

"Oh." I straightened in my chair and blinked down at my lap. "They think I'm too young and inexperienced to be training with them."

He nodded slowly and tapped a finger on the outside of the folder in his hands. "I see here that you've done well keeping pace with them—and that you've been spending what little free time you have studying in the library?"

"Yes." I swallowed.

"And what do you study?" His question sounded irrelevant, but some part of my mind searched for the trapdoor. What would my answer prove or disprove? Dante's tender eyes pulled the truth from me before I had time to evaluate it first.

"Everything," I said, my breath trembling. "I'm a sireless vampling, and this program isn't designed to cover the scion basics. So I'm learning them on my own the best I can."

My answer seemed to tug at his grin. "And how is that going, Ms. Skye?" he asked, coming around the desk between us to lean against the edge of it.

I shrugged. "Great, until tonight." I pressed my hands to my face. "God, Sonja…who could have done that?"

"That's what I intend to find out," Dante said.

It felt like I was being dismissed. I was training to be a Blood Vice agent, but I wasn't one yet. Still, it stung to be on the outside, especially when the crime was so personal. Sonja was my friend. She'd been left in the library, where everyone knew I would be.

"I don't feel safe here," I admitted.

Dante sighed. "I heard about the coffin in the pool. To be frank, I'm amazed that you didn't quit that first day. I certainly didn't expect you to last this long. You keep surprising me, Ms. Skye."

"I don't want to quit now." I frowned at him. "But I don't want to have my heart carved out in my sleep, either."

"I assure you, you are perfectly safe now that I'm here. Nothing will happen to you. I swear it." He reached out, his hand coming close to touching my chin before it diverted and squeezed my shoulder instead. Warmth emanated from his exposed arm where the sleeve of his dress shirt had been folded back. I could feel it on my cheek. It made me aware of how cold I was, and reminded me that I hadn't fed tonight.

"May I ask you a question?" I said as he released my shoulder and pulled away.

His eyes lit up. "Anything."

"Why *did* you allow me into this program if you didn't think I'd last?" I blushed, wondering if he'd heard about the circulating rumors in addition to the pool ordeal.

Dante folded an arm across his chest and propped his opposite elbow on it before pressing his knuckles against his chin. He gave me a thoughtful frown. "Most sireless vamplings would have been content to be granted the opportunity to beg for their lives, but you not only refused to grovel, you requested to be thrown on the frontline. I wanted to see how far that tenacity would take you. I still do."

A knock on the door abruptly ended our conversation.

"Enter," Dante called out.

"The other cadets are arriving, Your Grace," one of the guards announced from the hallway.

The duke nodded. "Escort Ms. Skye back to the crypt and bring Ms. Hanson in to be interviewed next." He gave me another of his charming, demure frowns. "My condolences on the loss of your friend."

"Thank you, Your Grace." I bowed my head before standing to leave.

Dante's guard followed me a few steps behind. He wasn't especially fancy or obvious. Just a plain, black suit that obviously hid several firearms. His looming presence was silent, but I felt the authority rolling off him, and it unnerved me.

"I haven't fed yet," I said to him over my shoulder. "Do you mind if we stop by the harem first?"

"Straight to the crypt," he said, voice low and warning. "Those were the orders. Besides, the harem has been cleared out."

"What?"

"It's for their safety."

I paused in the hallway, but only briefly before he nudged me to continue on. "We're on a base full of vampires. How the hell is that supposed to work?" I hissed.

The man snorted behind me. "Let the grownups worry about that, vampling."

A hollow pit formed in my stomach as we reached the crypt. The other cadets all turned to watch as I entered the room, Dante's guard close at my back. Their glares were less bothered tonight, edged more with cautious suspicion instead. I eyed each of them in turn, lingering a moment longer on Mic. Then I spotted another of Dante's guards in the corner of the room.

"Ms. Hanson." My escort waved a hand at her, beckoning her out of the room. "The duke would like a word with you."

Blair's eyes bulged, and she sucked in a sharp breath before frowning in my direction. She clearly assumed that I had pointed a finger at her. There wasn't time to explain that I hadn't—not that I was overly concerned with easing her anxiety. Not when she'd been the source of so much of my own since arriving at the bat cave.

Once Blair had departed, the others turned on me.

"What the hell is going on?" Emma wanted to know.

I glanced at the guard in the corner and pressed my lips together. The duke hadn't told me to keep quiet, but I knew that whatever I shared here would go straight back to him, so I had to consider my words carefully.

"Where's Sonja?" Andre asked next. He sat on the edge

of his bunk, elbows propped on his knees.

"Sonja is dead." My eyes fell on Mic again, searching for any trace of guilt.

"Don't fucking look at me like that," he spat, surprise and panic lacing his features. "You two were the only ones who stayed on base."

"The harem did, too," Andre injected, his mind initiating an internal investigation the same way mine had.

I shook my head. "I don't think a human could have…managed something like that."

Emma huffed and leaned back against the wall behind her bunk. She ran both hands through her short hair. "What a fucking mess." Her disgust seemed to extend to all of us. "This had better not terminate the program. I've worked too hard to get this far."

"We all have," Andre said, his eyes narrowing on Mic. "I didn't see you tonight, Novak. Where did you run off to?"

Mic's face flushed, and he stopped pacing the room. In a flash, he was standing before Andre, towering over him. "Shut your fucking face, Freeman," he growled, fangs extending.

Andre stood slowly, coming to his full height a good five inches taller than Mic. His callous eyes stared down at the vampire as his own fangs began to slide free, digging into his bottom lip.

The guard in the corner slipped a hand inside the fold of

his jacket, and we all froze. "Sit down, boys," he said calmly. "You'll all have your turn with the duke."

Andre and Mic parted and settled into their bunks. I did the same.

My heart was heavy, but I struggled with my grief over Sonja. I tried not to think about the friends and family who would undoubtedly be grieving her soon, too. I hadn't known her long, but losing that beacon of kindness in this place after being surrounded by so much loathing and ridicule…it was devastating. Still, something clenched in my chest, telling me not to show weakness in the company of predators.

We all stewed in silence until Blair returned. Andre was summoned next. Blair refused to speak to any of us as she climbed into her bunk. Even when Mic pressed her for details, she simply shook her head and lay down.

The interviews carried on, even as sunrise approached. Mic was last to be called out of the crypt. Nearly an hour passed, and he didn't return.

The guard in the corner swapped places with a human shortly before daybreak. I knew he was human because the panic and despair churning in my mind had activated the Eye of Blood, and the new guard faded behind the red screen while the vampire cadets in their bunks dotted my vision with bursts of color.

I fought dawn as it came for me, knowing some awful

fate lingered in the shadows, waiting for the cover of day to strike.

Chapter Fifteen

I woke with a start Sunday night, wondering why the overhead light in the crypt hadn't come on. When my head connected with a felt-lined panel, I had my answer.

Being in a coffin again set my heart off like a rabbit after hearing a gunshot. I pounded my fist against the box and gasped, suddenly unable to catch my breath. "Help!"

A muffled groan sounded nearby. "Get comfy, green fang. We're going to be here a while," Blair's annoyed voice echoed as if coming from another coffin.

I heard Andre grumble next. "Great."

"Mic?" Blair called out, hope and worry hiking her voice. "Emma?"

"Present," Emma answered dryly. "Now feel free to fuck off. I'll be meditating for the next three days."

"Mic?" Blair tried one more time. But he never answered.

We all fell quiet, and I wondered who else might be listening. I wondered how well the others had fed the night before. If this were the three-day coffin-lock trial as Blair had suggested, it would end up being four for me. Was that something that could even be done?

A few minutes later, I heard the crypt door hiss open, and Sergeant Sorano's voice greeted us. "Attention, cadets. I'm sure by now, you've realized that you're in coffins. You'll remain in them for three days to test your stamina. If, at any point, you reach your limit, you are free to *tap out* by telling the guard stationed in the room your name and household affiliation."

"Where's Mic?" Blair demanded.

"I'm not here to answer your questions, Ms. Hanson," Sorano snapped.

"Ma'am," I tried to catch her attention next. "I didn't feed yesterday. Will that be counted as my first night?"

"No. You'll be released when everyone else is—unless you'd like to share your name and household?"

I pinched my eyes closed and swore under my breath. "No, ma'am."

"I'd keep the hysterics to a minimum, too," Sorano added. "If you piss off Gerald, he has the authority to terminate your session and boot you out of the program."

The creak of the crypt door as it closed suggested that was all the explanation she'd be offering. We were on our own. Except for the deathly silent Gerald. Was he one of the duke's guards? I wondered, having nothing better to do. Was he kicked back on one of the empty bunks, reading? Going through our personal effects?

No one made a sound. Sorano wasn't one for issuing false threats, and testing the guard sounded on par with tapping out. The silence stretched on forever. I felt my wrist, searching for my watch so I could check the time, but it had been removed. The only way we'd be counting down our misfortune was by the rising and setting sun.

I pictured Blair pouting in her own box, and Emma attempting to meditate. Lotus position was a no-go, but I envisioned her hands folded over her chest, all Dracula zen. I wished I had my earbuds to pass the time. Instead, I closed my eyes and silently mouthed the meager Spanish I'd learned. I thought about the most recent things I had read in the library. Then I thought about the last few conversations I'd had with Sonja. A lump formed in my throat as I decided that maybe wasn't the best thing to contemplate at the moment.

I was no good at this game. Being alone with my thoughts never led anywhere pleasant. Every little anxiety came out to play. My mind wandered, stumbled back in history, and found the familiar face that served as the bittersweet backdrop of my consciousness.

My mother.

She was lying in a coffin, too. Some eight hundred odd miles away. Though she was, hopefully, more at peace than I was right now. If she were alive, I wondered what she would think of this new version of me, of my thirst for blood and the nocturnal hours I kept. Could she overlook those oddities and still be proud of me? Would she think I was on the right path? Was I doing the right thing here?

I couldn't tell anymore.

It was hard not to feel at least a little responsible for Sonja's death. Things I'd been too shocked to recognize or consider before came back to probe at my raw condition. Why hadn't Sonja told me she was going to stay behind? Had she just wanted some peace and quiet? Was she afraid I would badger her with my ignorant questions the whole time?

Even though I couldn't see anything beyond the inside of my own coffin, Mic's absence haunted me. He was a prick, through and through. And Sonja had pushed his buttons more than anyone else. But…I just couldn't imagine him going to such an extreme.

Every thought of Sonja conjured the grim image of how I'd found her. It was much too fresh in my mind to stave off for long. In the darkness, I could see her open, vacant eyes staring back at me. The raw wound in her chest was sloppy, like a hollowed-out jack-o-lantern. I'd never seen anything like it in my time as an officer. What alarmed me most, though, were the two neat puncture marks lining the right side of her throat, as if she hadn't struggled at all when bitten.

It didn't make sense. I'd asked Sonja about blood rituals between vampires, and she'd expressed mild distaste for the taboo practice. The act made sense between sire and scion, and there were even…*toys* to assist in the deed, like stainless steel fangs for half-sired imitation feeding. Blood sharing was less acceptable between vampires, but some mated couples chose to do it anyway. As for maintaining a healthy diet, vampire blood offered little in the way of sustaining another of the same species. Something about depleted platelets and oxygen levels.

There had been a serial killer noted in Kai's law class who'd fed from his own kind before killing them, a depraved power play. The wounds he'd left behind, pictured in our textbook, were ragged as a result of the victims' struggling. Not clean, tiny holes like those left on Sonja. Even if she had willingly let another vampire bite her, it was most certainly not Mic Novak.

The festering questions plagued me all night, though there was nothing I could do about any of it from inside a damned box. I longed for the training to be over, for the feel of a badge in my hand and the authority to do something worthwhile again. I was tired of being told to let others take the lead and sort things out. To not worry my pretty little head over it. That needed to change. Soon.

The ache in my stomach didn't let up, but as the sun drew closer to the horizon, I felt the pang of hunger punch more urgently, telling me that my window of opportunity was closing. I rubbed my eyes, trying to keep them open just a little longer despite my agony, feeling courageous and proud that I hadn't yet yielded and called out my name.

The next two nights were not so kind.

Chapter Sixteen

A vampire needs blood. It's one of the few truths even humans who are not in the fold seem to understand about the species. Immortal is such a fluid term. On the one hand, sure, a vampire could potentially live forever. But only if they drink human blood regularly, never went out in the sun, steered clear of silver, and didn't sustain too much heart or head trauma.

Mandy had warned me, shortly after we first met, that she'd heard of new vamplings who had gone full-on psycho after not feeding for a few days. I had less than six months behind me. Near the end of the coffin-lock trial, my greatest fear was that I would lose my mind before my stubbornness gave way and allowed me to tell the guard my name.

I nearly did tell him, but the jury was still out on how intact my mind remained.

The lights were too bright, and I was no longer in the crypt. I didn't remember being moved. I didn't remember waking after sunset. This felt a lot like a police raid in the dead of night, except I was on the wrong end of it.

"*Necesito sangre*," I rasped. My vision blurred in and out of focus. Shapes took form, liquid lines sharpening as if they'd been drenched in blood. The world was a sea of burning red, slowly draining away as I emerged from the mouth of hell.

"What's wrong with her?" someone asked.

"She hasn't had blood in three nights. What did you expect her to look like?"

"Jenna, can you hear me?"

Their voices were distorted as if they were underwater, or under all the blood just out of my reach. Where was it all dripping away to? I needed it. Desperation speared my heart. My stomach cramped, and I felt my lungs labor for my next breath.

A hand touched the side of my face, and then Sergeant Sorano appeared through the liquid haze. Her thumb slid over my cheek, and she pulled down the skin under my eye, shining a small flashlight at my pupil.

"Are you in there, Skye?" she whispered, real concern pinching her brow.

I made to nod, but my neck was so stiff. My jaw, too. I tried to move my arms next. My fingers trembled, and my elbows locked. I reached out of the coffin with all the grace of Frankenstein's bride. A dry croak whispered past my throat, and Sorano eased out of my path.

"You just have to make it to your donor, and you can have a drink," she said, eying the other bodies in the room.

My tunnel vision extended as I stepped out of the coffin, and I saw the base harem crowded around us, forming a narrow pathway that ended where Collins and Kai stood. I looked for Natalie and Sampson, but I didn't see them any-where in the room.

I shuffled a few steps toward Collins, still scouring the crowd for someone I could sink my fangs into. The eyeteeth ripped at my gums as I tried to lengthen them. A trickle of my own blood dripped onto my dry tongue.

"You're doing great," Collins said, waving a steady hand at me. "I'm right here."

I looked at him again, really taking in what the under-ground training had done. Despite the span of his shoulders being wider, he looked haggard. His skin was paler, but his hair was a shade darker. It was longer, too, hanging around his face in unkempt tufts. I'd only been coffin-locked for three days, but my memories of Collins on the force with his golden tan and military haircut had played more frequently through my mind than this new version of my friend. This was my fault. He wouldn't have been here if not for me.

I found my voice again just before I reached him. "Who?" The word was barely a breath from my lips.

"Me," he said as if it were obvious. "You're going to drink from me." He pushed the sleeve of his fatigue shirt up and thrust out his wrist. The thin scars from where he'd opened his flesh himself and bled into a cup for me were all healed now. They ran in an inch-wide row just beneath the swell of his palm.

"No," my eroded throat protested.

Collins nodded and tried to take a step closer to me, but Kai put an arm out to stop him.

"She has to do this herself. It's part of the trial." The vampire eyed me intently, as if trying to communicate something more pressing without spelling it out.

"Please," Collins begged, his wrist still held out before him. His eyes glossed over, and he swallowed. "You have to. You're so close."

You're so close. Was that a good enough reason to do it? My brain tried to launch a debate, but my stomach clenched, tugging me forward.

I thought again of Natalie, of how comfortable I'd become with her. When I fed from her wrist, I was thoughtful and gentle, creating as little pain and injury as possible. It had taken a few attempts to perfect the method, and a lot of advice and tips from her.

I didn't want to be thoughtful or gentle right now. I wanted to bite down on Collins' wrist like a savage dog and shake my head until his blood flowed over like a fondue fountain. I craved every last drop of it. My breath rushed in and out at the thought.

Collins frowned at Kai's arm where it lay across his chest. Then he glared up at the vampire. "I don't care how big and scary you are. I don't care if you kick us all out of the program.

That's my friend, and she needs me."

"Wait," I rasped. If I didn't get it together, all of this would be for nothing.

I took another step toward Collins and reached for him, my fingers skimming the button of his collar. Kai moved his arm away as I closed the gap. I tried again to remember how this worked with Natalie, but as my fangs strained to extend to their full length, I knew this wasn't going to be my best bite ever.

My fingers curled around Collins' forearm, and I noticed the skeletal sharpness of my knuckles and nails. My fatigue pants hung loosely around my waist. I blinked a few times and licked my cracked lips before glancing up at Kai.

"Four nights," I said softly. His brows knit together in confusion. "Ask Sorano. I haven't had blood for four nights. Make sure that goes in my file." I gave him a pointed stare as I sank my fangs into Collins' flesh.

Collins flinched, relaxing a few seconds later as my saliva coursed through his system. His chest swelled, and he made a soft noise in the back of his throat as I sucked at his vein. His blood felt hot, almost too hot on my tongue. It scorched my throat, but I swallowed as fast as I could, hoping it would help me regain my self-control in time.

I tried to take only as much as I needed to function on a more coherent level. Natalie and Sampson were around here somewhere. They could finish the job before I incapacitated Collins.

When I finally found the confidence to extract myself, I pulled away quickly, gasping as if coming up from a deep dive. Collins clasped his free hand over the seeping wounds I'd left and blinked at me, his eyes dreamy and unfocused. I hoped it was from the endorphins and not blood loss.

"Are we done here?" I asked Kai, giving him another neutral stare.

He nodded slowly, a cautious frown dragging at the corners of his mouth. Sorano stepped up beside him and handed over a clipboard for his signature. He gave it without taking his eyes off me for more than a split-second.

"Good job, Skye," Sorano said, sounding impressed. "You may spend the rest of the night with your harem. Be in the crypt by oh seven hundred hours for a program briefing." She handed my watch back to me, and I took it.

"Yes, ma'am." My teeth clenched as I struggled not to glare at her. Getting irate wouldn't do me any favors. Not if I wanted to make it through the remaining five weeks of the program.

Collins put an arm around my shoulders and steered me out of the room. We were in the harem hallway, the one opposite Natalie's room. As we shuffled across the long rug that led the way, Collins sagged more heavily against me, and we struggled to keep each other upright.

"I haven't eaten in a couple of days either," he admitted. "It's, apparently, a new trial in the human program—minor starvation and then donating blood, to prepare for emergency situations."

My fury bubbled irrationally before I could contain it, and my fangs began to emerge again. Collins noticed and squeezed his hand around the cap of my shoulder, holding me in place.

"I had the choice to quit. They didn't force it on me," he said.

Five weeks. Could I stand to look at these people that much longer? And not tear out their throats? I choked back angry tears and swallowed, trying to rein in the wrath. This had to be the bloodlust talking. I would feel better after I'd fed more, I hoped.

"This one," I croaked as we paused in front of Natalie's door with the glittery raven. Collins made a face, but he knocked with his free hand.

The door jerked open, and Natalie's beaming face greeted us, along with a burst of confetti from a cardboard funnel. Shiny cutouts of tiny, black bats and yellow crescent moons rained down on us.

"Congratulations!" she squealed. More voices echoed hers, and I spotted the other three members of my loaner harem behind her.

Mandy appeared next, pushing past Natalie to reach me. "Are you…okay?" She grabbed my hand and gave it a squeeze. Then her brow scrunched as she examined my thin fingers and arms.

"I just need to feed a little more," I assured her, attempting a small smile. That only seemed to distress her further until Natalie chimed in.

"Do you mind the audience?" she asked, already rubbing down her wrist with a wet wipe. "We can use Sampson's room if you'd like some privacy."

"No. Here's fine." I was far too hungry to fuss over modesty, and everyone in this room had shared blood with me before so it seemed silly to think I should hide from them.

Natalie shooed Cara down to the foot of her bed and made a spot for us. Mandy held tightly to my hand as Collins eased me across the room. He let Mandy take up his station at my side and headed for Natalie's dresser where a party tray of meats, cheeses, and olives had been laid out.

Natalie wedged herself in against the headboard since Mandy filled the space to my right, gripping my hand as if she might never let it go. She laid her head against my shoulder, her breath quivering with the beginnings of a sob.

"It's okay. I'm okay." I rested my head on top of hers, inhaling the earthy scent of her hair.

"Do you want me to…fill a cup?" she asked, sniffling.

"No, you're in training. Keep your strength," I said, turning to Natalie. She gave me a tender smile and held her wrist out to me.

I wasn't as ravenous as I'd been with Collins, but I definitely hadn't regained the bulk of my composure. To Natalie's credit, she didn't flinch or recoil when I bit down. Her breath was even, and she watched Mandy just as much as she observed me, as if concerned about stepping on toes within my true harem.

Mandy closed her eyes, and I heard her own breath hitch. She held me tightly, refusing to shy away even in the face of an exchange she had unwillingly endured too many times before escaping the Scarlett Inn. My blood boiled at the reminder that there were just as many scumbags in this world as the human one. It wasn't shocking, but it did reinforce a core reason why I was training at the bat cave in the first place.

After I'd released Natalie's arm, and apologized for my uncouth indulging, my next request was an update on current events. "Are the duke and company still on base?"

"They left yesterday," Sampson said. "They took the House Novak cadet with them. His donors are having their own party right now."

Natalie stood to tend to her wrist, and Sampson plopped down in her place, eager to divulge the gossip and his blood. Every donor was different, experiencing the chemical reaction in their own way. Sampson pinched nervously at the whiskers on his chin as I fed from the bend of his arm. His wrists were too ticklish.

"The creep claims he was with a hooker the night that girl from House Starling was killed," Sampson went on. He paused to wince when I unconsciously bit down harder at the mention of Sonja. "But no one else could confirm his alibi, and he'd already insulted Lord Starling once before, and was nearly locked up for it."

"What about everyone else?" I asked, wiping my mouth with the back of one hand.

Natalie reached for Sampson's arm and smeared a glob of her ointment on the holes I'd left in the crook of his elbow. "I think you were the first one they opened," she said. "I tried to tell Mr. Blueblood that you hadn't fed Saturday night, but I don't think he believed me. I think he just thought I was trying to help you cheat or something."

I ground my teeth and tried to push away the nagging suspicion that everyone in charge was conspiring to make training extra hard for me, the duke's pet vampling. He knew it, too. But I'd show them all. Tenacity, indeed.

"Cain is feeding Blair," Collins said around a mouthful of cheese. He balanced a paper plate heaped with food in one hand but continued to pick from the spread, stuffing more in his mouth as he spoke. "I'm guessing the other two in my unit are taking care of the remaining vamp cadets. We all signed on for the fast and bleed trial."

"Did the duke question you, too?" I asked him.

"No." He slurped at a cup of punch and swallowed. "Mandy and I were with Sergeant Carmichael the whole time. She took us to a piano bar. It was nice."

Mandy nodded against my shoulder and finally sat upright, rubbing her cheek with a sniffle. Her fatigue pants whispered against my own. The base harem donors had dressed up—or at least, Natalie, Sampson, and Cara had. Ned shrugged when he caught me staring at him.

"My shift up top begins in an hour," he said apologetically. "You wanna do me next before I have to head out?" Such a sweet talker, that one.

I stood and walked to him, testing out the steadiness of my legs. I was feeling much better, recovering remarkably fast. I guessed having the blood of three donors doing its magic at the same time would do that. Two more bites, and maybe I'd be able to shrug the hollow feeling eating at my core.

My thoughts turned to Roman, and my constant ache for him—not just for his blood, but also to have him near. Even brooding, his presence comforted and enlivened me. I wanted it now more than ever. There wasn't enough blood to satisfy that longing.

Ned's heavy breath reminded me of where I was and the

company I was in. I glanced up from his wrist, my fingers freezing mid-caress down the length of his arm. Everyone was staring. After my cheeks warmed, they quickly made a point to mind their own business.

Cara took Ned's place a moment later. "We bought you something," she said with a mischievous smile and a cueing glance behind me.

"Spoiler alert," Natalie chimed. She huffed with mock disappointment and waved her arm dramatically as she closed her bedroom door, revealing a deep red evening gown hanging on the backside.

Red lace folded to resemble flowers created the thin sleeves of the dress, and a thick band of material marked the empire-cut waist just under the bust. The pleated skirt was simple, the heavy fold of the material widening the hem enough to give it an elegant fullness.

I fingered the dress and frowned.

"Do you like it?" Natalie asked.

"What's it for?"

"The queen's All Hallows' Eve ball." She threw her hands up. "The one day cadets look forward to even more than graduation?"

"Right." I grimaced, remembering some detail or another from Roman's notes about getting to attend one of the queen's annual parties and being officially anointed by her.

"And this event is coming up soon?"

"In three nights," Natalie answered. "So you should probably try it on now, in case Cara needs to do any hemming."

"Right now?" My shoulders slumped forward.

"Collins and I get to go, too," Mandy said. "But we don't get to meet the queen. That's only for vamps."

"And our attire was picked out of a catalog by the sergeants so we'd all match," Collins added, a hint of revulsion in his voice. "I'd have packed a tux if I'd known." He gave me an accusing look as if I'd intentionally let him come unprepared.

I'd overlooked the frivolous details in Roman's notes—not that he'd included many of those—and focused on the more pressing material. *Sue me.*

I stayed in Natalie's room all evening, as Sergeant Sorano had said I could, even after the others left, including Mandy and Collins. They remained the longest, watching Cara fuss over my new dress as she tucked and pinned everywhere she deemed it needed to be taken in or hemmed. I thought it looked just fine as it was, but she insisted that it had to be perfect. She also showed me the diamond earrings and pendant necklace she had picked out to go with it.

I didn't know how I should feel about the party.

Everyone else seemed excited, but the queen was technically my great-great-grandsire. There was lots of potential for awkwardness. I imagined that the duke would be there, too, being royalty and all. Probably the whole cast of House Lilith, less the slain and exiled members.

Even more so than meeting the queen, I was nervous about crossing paths with Ursula, the mother of evil in my book. I didn't know whom else to expect, seeing as how I was a vampling on the outside of this fancy society, looking in. I wondered if Sonja's or Mic's sires would make an appearance. What would I say to either of them if our paths crossed?

At oh seven hundred, on the dot, I met up with the other cadets in the crypt. They seemed surprised to see me, especially Blair, but she kept her mouth shut as Sorano entered the room. She gave us each an appraising look before addressing us.

"I hope you've fed well," she said, folding her hands behind her back. "Training resumes tomorrow. We'll be measuring your rate of recovery over the next two nights. You'll get another break on Saturday to attend Her Majesty's All Hallows' Eve ball. Enjoy yourselves. It will be the last night off you'll have until graduation."

She left the room without addressing Mic's or Sonja's cleared-out bunks. None of the other cadets mentioned their absence either, though Blair spent the moments before sunrise staring at Mic's empty bed. I had a feeling she couldn't believe he was responsible either. But I didn't need to be told that one did not simply contradict the duke's judgment.

When it came to vampires, that brand of common sense was not a luxury. It was survival.

Chapter Seventeen

While all vampires in the United States were technically under the rule of House Lilith, the ones pledged to Blood Vice were held to a higher standard, entrusted with upholding vampiric law and order. So they were privileged with a royal address before taking their final oath after training. For the fall session, that meant receiving an invitation to the All Hallows' Eve ball hosted at the queen's estate in Evergreen, about an hour's drive from the bat cave.

Roman's notes had outlined the few holidays vampires celebrated. Halloween seemed a little cliché, but it was sacred to the fanged community, acting as a mass memorial to their dead, whose ashes were kept in the royal tomb under the manor—alongside anyone unfortunate enough to be serving a coffin-lock sentence.

In addition to All Hallows' Eve, there was Midwinter's Eve and Midsummer's Eve, the longest and shortest nights of the year. And then Imbolc Eve, on the first of February, when new scions were celebrated—and sometimes created for the symbolic nature of the holiday that I was still a bit fuzzy on.

The queen hosted celebrations for all four holidays, though the invitations were usually reserved for the noble families. Only vampires were permitted to attend the solstice celebrations, but the other two festivals were more inclusive, as made apparent by the presence of me and mine come Saturday night.

"I feel like a poodle in a tutu," Mandy grumbled. She yanked at the top of her prom-style ball gown, readjusting her breasts in plain sight.

"Keep it classy." I clicked my tongue at her.

The BATC party had arrived early, delivered via limo to the front steps of the queen's manor. We were the lowly newcomers tonight, expected to fawn over the important guests who were fashionably late. I was more interested in the venue. The castle-inspired architecture was overwhelming, with decorative stonework and arched windows lit by gothic torches lining the walkways and wide patios. The inside of the place was like a museum. I wondered if the queen actually lived here, or if this was just for social gatherings.

Collins adjusted his tie as we paused at an archway leading into the ballroom. "I'm going to find where they're hiding the refreshments," he said, nudging my shoulder.

Mandy gasped at the suggestion and clapped her hands together. "Be still, my heart."

The pair of them hurried off, abandoning me in the growing crowd of strangers. There was no one here I recognized other than the cadets from the bat cave, and we didn't exactly have a secret handshake. A fancy party wasn't going to change that. After the coffin-lock trial, they'd resumed their loathing avoidance of me. Except for Blair, who had upped her tormenting now that Mic wasn't around to offer up a distraction.

I sighed and leaned against a column near the dance floor, watching the others make small talk or bow to the fancier vamps as they strolled through the marble foyer at the front of the manor. Other than formal, there didn't seem to be a specific dress code. It looked very much like a costume party with the wide range of historic and modern attire. My best guess was that everyone wore clothing from the era of their first rising. I wondered what my dress revealed about me. Then I decided that I didn't care.

I was ready for the night to be over. I pushed away from the column, eager to find a quiet corner to retreat to until an icy blue gaze settled on me.

My breath caught at the sight of him—the confident square of his shoulders, the classic tuxedo, the slicked-back, white hair. He was a sharper version of the man I'd first met, an air of calm perfection about him that even the fanged guests paused to take notice of.

Roman seemed oblivious to the whispers. His face remained perfectly blank as he stalked across the room. I half expected him to breeze past me without a second glance. When he stopped a few feet away and held out his hand, my heart stopped.

"Dance with me."

It wasn't some coquettish request. Just a command. But I accepted, automatically slipping my hand in his. As soon as he'd pulled me a safe distance away from the others, I came to my senses.

"I can't dance," I whispered over his shoulder.

"They'll begin with a slow waltz. Just follow my lead. Can you do that?" His flat expression hadn't changed, but I heard the quip for what it was.

"Doubtful." I put my free hand on his shoulder. It felt good being this close to him after so long, though I could have done without the return of his callous façade.

Roman gripped my waist and froze, his chin tilted up and away from me. He stood statue-still as the musicians took up their seats and instruments on the lower tier before the stage. A cello played a low, solemn note, followed by a quivering bellow from an accordion. More couples took to the dance floor, taking their positions and waiting as Roman and I were. Then the music began in earnest, setting everyone into motion.

I fumbled a step after Roman, blushing when Blair's scornful laughter reached me. Roman pulled me around, giving her my back as we stepped deeper into the swaying crowd.

"You encourage her with your attention," he said through his teeth.

"I can't help it."

"Try." His eyes dipped for a brief second, flashing sincerely before his cool gaze returned. He stared off into the distance behind me. I tried to do the same, but it wasn't easy. His skin was warm beneath mine, and when his other hand squeezed my waist to direct me into an underarm turn, I gasped softly. If Roman noticed, he didn't let on.

"They are like sharks," he continued. "They only require a drop of blood to rouse, and you give it to them so easily. They need to be reminded that you are one of them."

"But you said not to make friends." I frowned and returned my hand to his shoulder.

"And I meant it." His familiar frustration made my heart cower. "They need to know that you're not prey."

Was that why he'd learned to be so guarded? Had the ignore-them-and-they'll-go-away tactic worked so well for him? Or was a half-sired considered harmless by most vampires?

The nervous discomfort he'd shown around me suddenly felt more meaningful. Was I not threatening enough to warrant the smokescreen treatment anymore? Or was I really so burdensome that he couldn't maintain it in my presence for long?

Roman's breath rushed across my cheek and tickled my ear. "They're distracted. Now's our chance."

Before I could ask what we needed a chance for, his hand tightened on mine, and he pivoted us right off the dance floor.

We dipped into an arched hallway off the ballroom. His fingers stayed laced with mine as he tugged me past several closed doors and an alcove holding a milky bust of a slack-jawed vampire. The model's extended fangs were made of ruby rather than marble like the rest of her. I wanted to pause and appreciate the beauty of it, but Roman's urgency pulled my attention ahead again.

We reached a bend in the hallway and turned, taking us fully out of public view. Roman pushed open a door and ushered me into the dark room. I wanted to ask if he knew where we were. And wasn't this area off-limits? Wandering aimlessly through a host's home was rude—and if my meager knowledge of vampire etiquette had taught me anything, it was that offending fancy vamps came with a hefty price tag.

"What are we doing?" I whispered as my eyes adjusted to the softer lighting, making out the ornately framed paintings decorating the walls.

"I don't know." Roman's conflicted voice stabbed at my heart.

I turned to him, finding his icy blue gaze focused on me. "Why are we in here?"

"I'm afraid to die," he confessed. His hand squeezed mine, and he placed my palm against his chest, right above his racing heart.

Hadn't he given me the cold shoulder for saving his life?

I didn't know what to say to him, and I didn't know where all of this was coming from.

"Roman—"

"I'm afraid to die," he said again, slipping his free hand behind my ear to comb his fingers through my hair. "Because I don't want it to change the way I feel about you."

My breath rushed out in a heatwave. "And…how do you feel about me?"

Roman barely let me finish before he answered by pressing his mouth to mine. His hand gripped the back of my head, pulling me in closer to him. A moan welled in my throat as his other hand found the small of my back.

For a bittersweet moment, I enjoyed the feel of him against me. How my heart jolted and fluttered. The way my body responded to his as if this were nature's grand plan finally coming together. But that's all this was. Nature. Pheromones and hormones we had both surrendered to like primitive creatures.

When we finally tore away from each other, limbs shaky and breaths labored, I asked the obvious question. "This is because we shared lifeblood, isn't it?"

"Twice," Roman said.

"I knew it was too good to be true. I mean, obviously. You can't stand me, especially after I—"

"Jenna." A tendon in his neck strained as he looked away

from me, but then his mouth found mine again, and I couldn't find the will to resist. Biology be damned. We were falling down a steep cliff, our tether snapped and dangling far above. There was no clawing our way out of this.

I raked both hands through his hair and then locked my arms behind his neck, mewling like a cat in heat. Roman made his own noises, deep in his throat. He backed me into the wall and ran his fingers down my ribcage, his hips digging in above mine as our breaths grew more ragged.

When he pulled away, I struggled against him, a desperate need filling me. The tips of my fangs were slowly extending, though I tried to suck them back in as I pleaded with Roman.

"I don't care," I whispered, my lips trailing the side of his throat. "I don't care how or why we feel this way. I want you."

He tucked his chin over my head and crushed me to his chest, shushing my begging. "Listen," he said. The muffled music that had followed us from the ballroom shifted, and a regal fanfare of strings sounded. "The royal family is arriving. We have to go."

I swallowed and blinked back disappointed tears while Roman straightened his jacket and smoothed his hair back into place the best he could. He gave me a tender, sad smile and touched my face, rubbing a thumb under my bottom lip.

"Your lipstick." He gasped softly. "I'm afraid…"

"That you're wearing most of it?" I finished with a

clipped, humorless laugh. Roman flushed and reached for his own mouth, but I beat him to it, fingering away the smears of red splotches I'd left on him. "What are we going to do?" I asked, not sure I wanted to know the answer.

Roman cupped his hands around mine, pulling them away from his face so he could kiss my knuckles. His worried eyes searched mine. "We're going to get through tonight. Then you're going to get through the rest of your training."

"And after?" I whispered, leaning in as if to kiss him. Roman began to lean forward to meet me and then stopped, blinking stiffly.

"We'll figure that out once you come home," he said, squeezing my hands until my gaze lifted from his swollen lips to meet his eyes. "We can't afford to be sloppy tonight. There are too many eyes eagerly awaiting a glimpse of the orphaned vampling the duke has shown favor to."

He brushed a curl off my shoulder and smoothed my hair down my back, a despairing attempt to erase the evidence of our tryst. I frowned at him, wondering if he'd prefer to erase the memory of it, too. This was a disaster. I thought of Vanessa, and a fresh wave of guilt and bitter envy washed over me, souring my stomach.

"Ready?" Roman asked, holding his arm out to me like a proper gentleman.

I didn't want proper. I wanted him to take me right here

in the dark gallery, with all the brooding paintings watching us. But I relented and took his arm, steeling my face for the masses as he had done.

We left the gallery with no one the wiser. But as we made it back to the ballroom, his confession boiled to the surface of my mind, no longer muted by the pulse of our desire.

He was afraid to die because he was afraid it would change the way he felt about me. He knew. I wondered for how long. Had he known what he was doing when he'd fed me his blood last summer?

Roman let go of my arm as we rounded the corner and emerged into the ballroom, though he stayed close to my side. Several pairs of keen eyes took note of us, but no one introduced his or herself. We were far beneath any station warranting special attention. Roman seemed more bothered by the slight than I was.

"His Grace, the Duke of House Lilith," announced a doorman in colonial garb, complete with a powdered wig and buckle-topped shoes.

Dante entered through the foyer. I hardly recognized him in his blue, Civil War-era coat. The garment hung to his knees, with two rows of shiny gold buttons spanning the entire length of his chest. More buttons shone at his cuffs, and gold embellishments decorated his shoulders. A felt Hardee hat rested on his head, with a bright red feather tucked into the band.

He paused in the archway that connected the foyer to the ballroom, his eyes searching the crowd. The guests bowed lower, and I was suddenly aware that I was the only one standing upright besides him. Roman's hand found mine and jerked me into an impromptu curtsey.

Heat rushed up my neck and into my face, but as I stole another glance at the duke, I saw a small grin twitch across his lips. Then it was gone, hidden beneath a staunch disguise for the predatory masses.

Roman was right. They were sharks. And if someone as powerful at Dante feared bleeding in these familiar waters, what chance did I stand as the new fish in the pond?

"You must pay better attention," Roman hissed in my ear as the murmur of the crowd resumed. "One wrong move, and you won't be leaving here tonight."

"I don't need a babysitter." I frowned at him, feeling the flush in my skin grow more uncomfortable. I was probably as red hot as the dress I wore.

Roman lifted a skeptical eyebrow and released my wrist. He pushed the folds of his jacket back and tucked his hands into the pockets of his slacks as if to prevent himself from accidentally touching me.

More eyes snagged on us now. I wondered what they were waiting for. How far had the rumors spread? Did they expect me to tail after the duke and the small lot of guards surrounding him?

A few moments later, Lord Starling arrived. As the doorman announced him, I turned to get a better look. I knew it was ridiculous to expect a familial resemblance, but it still surprised me when an elderly Asian man entered the foyer. His white kung fu jacket looked out of place among all the darker colors flooding the room.

"You're staring," Roman whispered. The worry straining his hushed voice didn't translate in his expression. His guard was up again, eyes steadily observing the sharks in the room without appearing too interested in any one particular guest.

"Is that Sonja Starling's sire?" I pressed.

Roman tilted his chin toward me and lowered his voice. "Her grandsire. His scion, Sonja's sire, is not in attendance. I hear she had to be coffin-locked to contain her…mourning."

"I should say something to him."

"No, you should not." His voice was even, but the authority was there, hidden in the way he stiffly enunciated each syllable.

I set off across the ballroom anyway, feeling Roman's presence at my back. Another guest had just departed from greeting Lord Starling, and he turned as I approached, curiosity puckering his brow.

"I'm sorry for your loss," I said before Roman could

intercept.

The old vampire regarded me with dark, appraising eyes. "And you would be?"

"Jenna Skye, a BATC cadet in the vampire program. House Zajalvo," I added when his frown deepened.

"Zajalvo's orphan?" His bushy eyebrows lifted at the revelation.

"Yes, sir." I dipped my head politely.

"I tended to a harem donor of his once," he said. "Lovely girl, though her English was terrible—worse than mine when I first came to this country." His face softened at the memory but hardened when his focus returned to me. "I was under the impression he preferred donors from his homeland."

I lowered my eyes, sensing the bait. "I don't know why he picked me, sir. I just wanted to express my condolences. Sonja was kind, and even though our time together was short, I considered her a friend."

Lord Starling frowned, but he offered me a conceding nod. "Then perhaps you know who is responsible for her true death? I do not believe the Novak *spawn* capable of such a bold slight."

Blair's obnoxious chortling drew my eyes over Lord Starling's shoulder, but I quickly refocused my attention, remembering Kai's warning about unproven accusations only leading to more trouble. "I wish I did."

"Her Majesty, the Queen of House Lilith," the doorman announced, ending our conversation. We all turned toward the foyer entrance.

With a name like Lili, I'd expected a petite girl, one as deceptively angelic as Scarlett. I'd prepared myself for the little terror's doppelganger. So when everyone bowed toward a tall, dark, and handsome woman, I was stunned immobile.

Her bronze skin glowed in the candlelight. The high cheekbones and strong jaw gave her a masculine sharpness, but the almond eyes and full lips were a Helen of Troy brand of beauty. How many vampires in this room were willing to die for that face alone?

A crown set with rubies and onyx rested on top of her head, holding up a nest of dark braids. Her neck and shoulders were bare, but I suspected it was to highlight the splendor of her headpiece. The massive dress she wore resumed with the extravagance. It was a deep, crimson red embroidered with black roses and swirling designs. Layered skirts trimmed with black lace blossomed at her waistline. The topmost skirt was bustled at two points in front, and under the hitched hem flowed a mass of black tulle. The dress hovered just above the floor, perfectly tailored to enhance the silence as she glided into a room.

Roman's fingers found mine again and squeezed hard, dragging me down into a deeper curtsey before Lili's head canted our way. She didn't comment on my sloppy, delayed genuflection, but her eyes grazed our touching hands.

Once she'd passed through the ballroom, swarmed by an entourage of attendants and personal guards, two servants opened a pair of decorated double doors leading into a separate area. Only after the queen had exited the crowd did everyone rise and begin speaking again.

"Kai and Sorano will expect you to line up soon," Roman said. "Don't get stupid in there. Bow long and low, and say 'Thank you, Your Majesty.' after she anoints you. Nothing more."

"Or what? Off with my head?" I gave him a teasing sneer, but there was no humor in his expression.

This was going to go great. I could already tell.

Chapter Eighteen

Back when I was a rookie patrol officer, I'd done a lot of random jobs that required a light police presence—supervising pro-life protests outside women's clinics, searching a parade crowd for a missing kid, breaking up fights at rock concerts, and once, I'd even been asked to work a pop culture convention, where fans stood in line for hours just to have their picture taken with their favorite actor or comic book artist.

Waiting in line to see the queen felt a lot like that. Of course, I somehow doubted she'd be too keen on striking a pose for a photo op. The wait time seemed even longer because I was by my lonesome. Roman, Mandy, and Collins weren't being granted an audience. Vamps only. Lucky me.

I waited my turn between Andre and Emma, finishing off the long procession ahead of us. The lords and ladies from the noble households got to go first, each eager to offer their personal acknowledgment to the queen and receive her attention in turn. I imagined they got more time with her than what the cadets would be allowed, too. For all I knew, she was taking the time to play a game of checkers with each of her favorite subjects.

The two servants at the entrance to her room immediately closed the doors behind guests as they entered, and the previous guest departed through a smaller side door down the hallway Roman and I had used to access the gallery where we'd necked like horny teenagers.

A shameful, erotic thrill pulsed through me every time I thought of him. I looked around, wondering where he'd gone. Wondering if there would be more time after seeing the queen to find another hidden nook…

My fantasizing was stunted by the sight of Cain Davis's fishy, gray eyes. The half-sired cadet watched me from where he reclined against the far wall, waiting like an obedient dog as Blair made small talk with the fanciest guests. She was doing a fair job of hiding her distress over Mic's situation—if she'd ever cared at all. The way her fingers grazed the hand of another vampire made me wonder if she'd already decided it was time to move on. Or if maybe that was the doting sire Sonja had spoken of, the one she'd insinuated Blair was sleeping with.

Emma's tight breath snapped my attention back to the line. Her simple, black dress would have been stunning in a human crowd, but it blended into the background amongst all the finery draping the guests at the queen's manor. Her wrists, neck, and ears remained bare, but her short hair was held back by a pair of white gold hairclips, the only bit of sparkle in her ensemble. She shuddered and closed her eyes before taking another sharp breath. The sound grated on my own nerves.

"Are you okay?" I asked, touching her arm. She shrugged me off with a glare.

"Wonderful. You're up." Her chin jerked ahead.

I spun around as Andre's backside disappeared through the double doors. Another servant who matched the doormen addressed me with a bored, straight face. "Sign here."

He held a large guest log with silver-gilded pages across one arm, wedged between his elbow and wrist. With his free hand, he offered me a thick quill. I took it and signed in the same fashion as those before me had, listing my full name, house affiliation, and sire. As I finished, the double doors began to part again.

Well. That escalated quickly.

I wasn't prepared. My panic had been a dull nag in the back of my mind until this moment. One of the doormen cleared his throat and stared at me. I stepped inside at his cue and folded my hands over my stomach as I assessed the new scene. Once again, Andre's backside caught my attention, and I watched him exit as I inched farther inside.

The throne room was straight out of a fairytale. The queen sat in a chair on a raised platform angled in the corner. More of the colonial servants were stationed around her— one behind the throne holding a stack of white silk, another at her side holding a shiny platter, and a third near the smaller exit into the hallway.

There were also several men in more modern suits like Roman's. *Vampires*, I thought as my blood vision made an appearance. An elite handful of seasoned agents served in a direct capacity as personal bodyguards to the royal family. It was the kind of promotion I couldn't even dream of setting my sights on until I had a hundred years behind me on Blood Vice. As it stood, I wasn't sure I wanted the honor. *Your Grace* this and *Your Majesty* that would drive me mad in no time, I was sure of it.

The duke was in the throne room, too, standing erect to the left of the dais, his hand resting on the hilt of his sword. He opened his free arm toward the queen, encouraging me along. I quickened my pace, hurrying to the foot of the steps where I curtseyed as low as my heels would allow. After a few uncomfortably long seconds, the queen's servant with the tray relieved me.

"Rise and approach the crown," he said.

I climbed the few steps, knees shaking and eyes roving the room as if I couldn't decide where I should be looking. The servant held up a gloved hand once I'd come close enough.

"Kneel," he instructed.

It was awkward in the dress, but I obeyed, hobbling down to my knees. When I was in an acceptable position, the queen took an ornate dagger from the tray, and the servant reached behind her to fetch a square of white silk from his associate. They'd done this a time or two before, apparently.

The queen pressed the blade to her finger, and a single drop of dark blood welled on the tip. She offered it to me, stretching her hand out in a silent summon to lean closer. I did, and when she pointed at my lips, I understood the command and opened my mouth. She tapped her finger lightly on the end of my tongue.

With this blood, I anoint thee mine forevermore.

The honeyed, feminine voice sent goosebumps crawling over my skin, only the queen hadn't spoken. As her drop of blood slid down my throat, the room faded into darkness around us, and I glimpsed a flash of her in a different light and time.

She was a woman then as she was now, but she wore a simple, colonial dress that she observed in an oval hand mirror. That *I* observed through her eyes. This was a distant memory of the queen's. Paranoia and panic tightened my throat, but I couldn't move. I was an unwilling voyeur.

The queen, Lili, touched two marks on her neck and frowned. "Will this fade when I die?" she asked, her voice much softer than before.

Another woman stood behind her, reflected in the looking glass. Long, strawberry blond hair flowed over her shoulder. She grinned at Lili, at *me*, and her liquid laughter sent a tremor through my veins. When she spoke, I recognized her voice as the first one I'd heard. It hadn't been Lili at all.

"It will be gone by nightfall this eve," she answered. She stood and came up behind Lili, delicately moving her dark hair aside to take a closer look at the girl's neck. She smiled at her handiwork and laid a soft kiss on the twin wounds.

Lili shuddered as she turned to face the woman. "I'm ready, my queen."

My queen. Lilith. Lili's sire.

Lilith pressed her hands to either side of Lili's face and tilted her head to one side. I felt my own head move with the motion, felt her fingers dig into my scalp. Her fangs extended methodically, and I lost sight of them as Lili closed her eyes—the eyes I'd borrowed. But I felt the sharp ache when Lilith bit down on the girl's neck, just below her ear. I heard the crunch of tendons and smelled the tang of blood.

And then I was back in the present. The queen watched me carefully from her throne. I blinked up at her before lowering my head again, feigning reverence in order to hide my shock.

What the hell was that? My mind grappled for an explanation. Was it some trick of the queen's? Did everyone experience the bite down memory lane when they tasted her blood? Hopefully, Roman would know what it all meant.

The manservant handed over the silk handkerchief, and

the queen wiped her finger, leaving a small smear of red across the white. She wiped the end of her blade next, leaving a second line not far from the first, about the distance between a pair of fangs. Her servant folded the silk into a tidy square and presented it to me with a bow, and then waved his arm toward the arched exit.

"Dismissed."

The little ritual reminded me of my high school graduation. *Take your diploma, smile for a picture, and move along. We don't have all day, kids.* But hey, what did I care? Everyone was more interested in the after-party anyway. And right now, I was more concerned with dodging the queen's piercing gaze.

"Thank you, Your Majesty," I said, remembering Roman's advice. I rose up off the platform with as much grace as a gorilla, doing my best not to step on the hem of my gown, and made my way down the steps.

Emma was already progressing across the room toward the queen. She looked more resolved, more confident than she had in line. I watched her over my shoulder as I slipped off toward the exit, my bloody handkerchief clenched in one fist. Emma moved faster than I had, and the queen was already drawing fresh blood before I reached the door.

That's when Emma struck. She rose up off her knees in one fluid motion, leaning at an angle as if stumbling. One hand seized the queen's elbow, and Emma thrust her full weight into the woman's arm as her other hand repositioned the wrist holding the dagger.

The blade penetrated the queen's chest, sinking in to the hilt. From my angle near the exit, I saw the tip of it protrude from her back and dig into the throne chair. The queen gasped violently, her mouth opening and closing without making words.

An instant of confused terror struck everyone in the room—everyone except Emma. The vampire slipped a hand into her hair, ripping one of the brooches free. It cracked open in her palm, and a powdery substance sifted from its edges. She held it in front of her mouth and blew the contents into the queen's gaping face.

Dante was the first to break the spell of silent horror that had befallen us. He reached the throne as Emma made her escape, catching the queen in his arms as she tumbled from her chair. Her hand still clasped the handle of the dagger. She choked violently, her face ashen from the strange powder, and the whites of her eyes turning black.

Emma fled toward the exit I blocked. The skirt of her dress was wadded in one hand. She looked right past me, not even acknowledging my presence, just as she'd done a thousand times in the bat cave.

"Stop her! Bar the doors!" Dante ordered. The command was meant for the agents in the room, but I was closest, and growing closer as Emma neared me.

My instinct was to attempt one of the takedowns we'd learned in class—but she'd trained alongside me and would be expecting that. My hesitation didn't leave room for a more eloquent plan. As Emma tried to dodge past me, I snagged the back of her dress.

The material ripped but held, slowing her down. She swung her free arm in a wide arc, clocking me across the cheek. I grunted at the impact, but I refused to let go. As soon as my head snapped around, I tackled her. Her face hit hard, and her chin made a sickening crack as it connected with the marble floor. Still, she fought against me.

In our dresses, we probably looked like feuding pageant rejects. Several of the agents had drawn their weapons. They circled us with pinched brows.

"Stand down!" one of the men shouted. For a moment, I wasn't sure if they were making the request of Emma or me. When she reached for her remaining hairpin, I didn't care.

I grabbed Emma's wrists and pushed them to the floor, pressing my chest across her shoulder blades to hold her down. She shrieked and threw her head back, cracking her skull into my nose. I bled instantly. The sight triggered my fangs, and before I knew what I was doing, I'd bitten the back of Emma's neck.

I sucked hard, hoping to weaken her enough that I could

safely dismount without getting dusted. When her struggling lessened and her arms grew slack, I released her long enough to rip the brooch out of her hair.

One of the agents held his hand out for it as I stood, and two others swooped in to cuff Emma. Her blood had shaken me, delivering another glimpse into the past. I didn't have time to dwell on it right now. Not with the queen wheezing on the platform, taking her dying breaths in Dante's arms.

I took a step toward them, but one of the agents cut me off, the end of his gun trained on my face.

"Let her pass," Dante ordered. The agent grimaced, but he obeyed.

"What can I do?" I begged him. "Should we call for her harem? Will that fix…this?" I looked down at the queen's unseeing, black eyes. A vein in her brow pulsed with each breath she croaked.

Dante's jaw flexed. He shook his head. "She's been poisoned with silver. It will impede healing. She will not recover in time to survive this mortal wound." His voice broke, and a tear flicked from his lashes as he blinked up at me.

"I'm sorry." I didn't know what else to say. Too many thoughts and questions crowded my mind. I was forever ignorant in these matters—but that was why I had taken to studying in the library. That was why I'd hung on Sonja's every word.

"The blood of one's enemy," I said, remembering the archaic blood rituals book she'd explained the science of to me.

"What?" Dante looked at me as if he feared I'd perhaps inhaled some silver myself.

"To counteract silver poisoning," I clarified. "The blood of one's enemy."

He closed his eyes and blew out a disappointed sigh. "That's an old bat's tale."

"No, there's truth in it—Sonja Starling explained how it works. Trust me." I folded my hands together, pleading with him.

Across the room, Emma sagged between two guards, looking miserable and defeated. Her glare was directed at me, but it was filled with less malice than I'd expected. Until she understood what I was proposing.

"Trust me," I said again. "What do you have to lose by trying?"

Dante considered me with wide, helpless eyes. "Nothing." He motioned for the agents to come closer. "Bring her here."

"Your Grace," one of the men protested. "I would be remiss if I didn't remind you that the Vampiric High Council will consider this a breach of their authority."

The duke's demeanor changed, and I didn't recognize the face he offered the defiant agent. "You are employed by

House Lilith, not the council." His voice was whisper-soft, but the threat in it sent a chill over my skin. "Must I repeat myself?"

The agent answered by dragging Emma forward. Alarm flashed through her eyes, and she began to pant as Dante extracted the dagger from the queen's chest.

"I had no choice," Emma sobbed. "I'm sworn to serve my sire."

Dante didn't waste any time. He lashed out, slicing the dagger across her throat so quickly that I flinched.

The two agents holding Emma's arms positioned her over the queen, allowing the dark blood seeping from her throat to enter the queen's open mouth. It filled quickly, staining her teeth red as the liquid overflowed and ran across Lili's cheek to touch her earlobe. I feared they were too late, but then she swallowed.

An air bubble swelled up between her lips and popped as she swallowed again. Her throat continued to work, and soon, the black in her eyes retreated. Emma shivered as her own eyes took on that darkness that signaled she was near death. The agents made to move her away, but I reached out, touching one's arm.

"The last bit is the most vital," I said, ignoring the patronizing look he gave me.

The remainder of Emma's blood dripped free, and she

hung motionless, fully spent and unsalvageable. If she weren't dead, she would be soon enough.

I knew I should have cared that we'd just played executioner with a suspect. That she would not see a fair trial. But being present for the crime, I couldn't bring myself to feel much guilt. Not as the queen was roused from the brink of death.

"Lili?" Dante brushed his fingers down her bloodied cheek. "How do you feel?"

She groaned and glanced around the room, taking in the anxious faces as she answered. "I feel…like our guards might be overpaid."

The duke laughed at her words, but the agents in the room seemed to bristle with shame and resentment. One glared at me as if my interference had robbed him of the opportunity to play hero.

"Fetch the queen's harem," Dante ordered one of the costumed servants. The man hurried from the room, stealthily slipping past one of the double doors.

The queen let Dante help her up, extending her opposite hand out to me. I took it, feeling awkward at the sudden change in our dynamic. I guessed saving someone's life could have that effect.

The hole in her chest was still a raw wound, but it had stopped gushing. She didn't even wince as she probed it with her fingers. The blood painting her cleavage had also darkened the front of her dress, ruining the elaborate material, but she adjusted her crown regardless.

"It seems I owe an orphaned vampling my life." She sounded surprised, but not entirely upset. I was sure there were plenty of people more notable than I who had defended her through the centuries—even if her current guards were less than valiant. "What would the last living scion of House Zajalvo have of her queen?"

"A sire." My answer was sudden, widening Lili's eyes with displeasure. She hadn't even fully reseated herself in the throne. "If Your Majesty pleases," I added, bowing my head.

Addressing royalty still felt awkward, and the massive respect House Lilith demanded was a stark contrast to how the country's human leaders were regarded.

"A sire," Lili mused. She touched the trail of blood running down her cheek and then rubbed her thumb and index finger together. The servant with the stack of silk cloths knelt at her side and offered them up to her. She handed me one and took another for herself, dabbing it across her cheek first and then her chest. "Most vamplings are all too eager to outgrow their elders, and here you are, using up a royal boon to request one."

My palms itched as I wiped at the blood smeared under my nose and down my chin. I didn't say anything more as I

watched her consider her answer. This wasn't a fairytale scenario. She hadn't promised me whatever I wanted. She'd
simply asked what I would have of her. I'm sure she didn't
expect me to ask for a bath bomb or anything so trivial, but
maybe a sire was a taller order than she was capable of arrang-
ing?

"It will take some time," she said. I looked up, confirming
that she was serious and not just teasing me. My vampiric ignorance had been met with so much mockery since I joined
the fold. "I'll announce your replacement sire on Midsummer's Eve when we celebrate the returning darkness. Add her
name to the guest list," she said to another servant in the
room.

"Thank you, Your Majesty." I bowed my head again and
tried to breathe through my nose before I hyperventilated.

"Thank *you*," she replied, bypassing the servant who had
acted as her mouthpiece. The words seemed unfamiliar to her,
but she offered them sincerely.

"I'll escort you back to the party," the duke announced as
a swarm of humans entered the throne room. From their
matching robes, they were obviously the queen's harem.

I gave the queen a final, appreciative nod before taking
Dante's offered arm. The agents had lain Emma's body
against the far wall and covered her with a sheet. As we exited
into the hallway, the duke cleared his throat, drawing my

attention away from the contained scene.

"Will the party really go on?" I asked, a little unnerved by the way they were so ready to cover up such a serious incident.

"The assault will be announced in an official capacity after the queen is fully recovered," Dante said under his breath. He covered my hand where it lay on his arm. "It would be greatly appreciated if you kept what just happened to yourself until then."

I met his gaze and swallowed. "Of course."

"Thank you for your service."

"What about Mic?" I asked as he began to pull away.

"Excuse me?"

"Mic Novak. Is he coffin-locked for a crime that's likely Emma's?" I might have been able to overlook the improvised death of House Kincade's scion for the time being, but Mic…that wasn't justice. Being an asshole was not a crime in and of itself.

The duke inhaled a tense breath and had the decency to look ashamed. "I'll make a call and have him released immediately," he said. "Is there anything else, Ms. Skye?"

I shook my head, aware that I was toeing the line of insubordination again. I was good at that. "Thank you, Your Grace."

"Enjoy the rest of the party."

He left me in the dark hallway and retreated back inside

the throne room, closing the heavy door behind him. The dismissal struck a nerve I hadn't known I possessed.

I should be in there with them.

The irrational thought came to me as I headed for the ballroom. I couldn't confess the familial pull. Just like I couldn't admit to having the Eye of Blood, nor what it had shown me through Emma. It wasn't just for improved night vision or discerning vampires from humans. It connected to the moment of a vampire's origin, revealing their sire. And Emma's sire had just arrived.

She stood in the foyer, draped in a velvet cloak with a high, Victorian collar that framed her face. Soft, brunette curls were piled on top of her head, and a golden circlet lay across her brow. Her sharp eyes matched the emerald of her dress.

"His Highness, the Prince and Her Grace, the Duchess of House Lilith," the doorman announced.

I hadn't even noticed the man a step behind Kassandra. As the guests bowed to them, I again faltered, forgetting my place, and was the last to yield. When I looked up, they were gone. Disappeared to some other corner of the manor.

I had to find Roman. He was the only one I could tell my secrets, and I hoped like hell he would know what to do.

Chapter Nineteen

I found him in the gallery, waiting for me. He'd had the same brilliant idea to steal away the rest of the night without words or thoughts, just reckless passion. And here I was, coming to ruin it all.

"The cadet from House Kincade just attempted to assassinate the queen." My words rushed out in a heated whisper. "Except she's not really a Kincade—she belongs to the duchess, Kassandra. I bit her, and I saw… I saw…" I panted, grasping for the right words.

"You bit the duchess?" Roman asked, a horrified light filling his eyes.

"No," I hissed. "Emma—the cadet—I bit her. Kassandra is her sire. She's the one behind the assassination. And she's here. *Now.*" I pressed my hands to the sides of my face and then winced.

"What happened to you?" Roman's fingers grazed my chin as he examined my aching cheek. The silk cloth the queen offered me had erased the blood, but there was still a bruise to contend with.

"I stopped Emma from escaping," I said, pulling my face away from him. "Are you listening to me? Kassandra is trying to kill the queen." I gripped the lapels of his jacket. "What do we do?"

"You only know this because of the Eye of Blood?" he asked, finally catching up.

"Yes."

"Then we do nothing."

"What?" I hissed.

"Do you enjoy being alive and free?" He squeezed my shoulders in his hands, his gaze leveling with mine. "Because I enjoy you being alive and free. And I'd like you to stay that way."

"But—"

"It's not your place," he insisted, giving me a gentle shake. "They will never recognize you as one of them, and even if you survive the confession, you will not survive their enemies. Is that what you want?"

I lowered my eyes, trying to accept what he was telling me. It was the obvious truth, but it still hurt, however irrational the sentiment was. *Even after everything that had just happened?* I wondered. It was all over and done with so fast, I began to doubt it had transpired at all.

"The queen is alive and well?" Roman asked. I nodded. "Then her guards will be more vigilant and watchful tonight." He kissed my temple and then my cheek, moving downward until he reached the curve of my neck.

My breath hitched, and I closed my eyes, trying to forget everything, at least long enough to enjoy Roman for the short time I would have him tonight.

"Did the queen offer you riches for your loyal service?" his playful voice cooed in my ear.

"She did." I sighed and reached my arms around his waist. "I'll have a new sire by Midsummer."

Roman jerked away from me. "What? Why?"

I blinked at him. "Because that's what I asked for."

"Why would you do such a stupid thing?" His voice rose, but he quickly lowered it before stalking a tight circle around the gallery. "Zajalvo was perfect. With him being dead, you were free to live as you chose. Now you'll be under the thumb of whomever the queen decides to subject you to."

"And what if I need that?" I hugged myself, staving off a bitter cold that was quickly settling in my bones. "What if I can't do this alone?"

He cupped a hand at his chest. "You have me."

"Really?" I scoffed. "Because you've been so much help?"

His face screwed up in frustration. "I gave you my training notes even after you went against my advice and applied for the program."

"And you completely ignored me the two weeks before that."

"Because you—" He blew out an angry breath and placed his hands on his hips. "You're impossible." My heart plummeted. But then he was on me again, pulling my body against his while his mouth sought mine. The music from the ballroom grew louder, disguising our unrefined noises.

We were a match made in purgatory, both stuck in our own paths where they intersected. But for how long?

That was a question for another night, I decided as Roman pushed me against the wall of the gallery, and my blood boiled with desire.

A regal party was no place to consummate…whatever it was that Roman and I had going. I didn't know what to call it. I hadn't cared if it had a name at all while his lips had razed every inch of my exposed skin. I was flustered and achingly unfulfilled by the time the cadets were expected to line up outside.

I was a little embarrassed that I'd yielded so quickly, allowing Roman to brush away my concerns over House Lilith affairs. But he'd been right. There was nothing I could do without offering myself up as a sacrificial lamb.

I didn't see Kassandra again. Of course, I didn't see much of anyone from inside the gallery.

"What happened to you?" Mandy asked, snuggling in between Collins and me. "I looked everywhere."

"Not everywhere." I grinned.

My senses returned to me slowly in the chill outside the manor. Sergeant Sorano stared me down as if she knew what I'd been doing all night. She had at least half the story, I realized when the limos began to pull up to the curb, and Andre questioned where Emma was.

"Ms. Kincade has been dismissed from the program. She will not be returning with us," Sorano said, still watching me.

The drive back to the bat cave was quiet. With Roman no longer there to take my mind off everything, my thoughts circled back to Emma. If her end goal was to assassinate the queen, why did she have to kill Sonja? Did she discover Emma's evil plan? Something still felt…missing from the equation.

Collins and Mandy eyed me curiously, but with Carmichael, Andre, and the other wolf cadet sharing a limo with us, they knew better than to ask. Though they did pull me aside as the others headed off to the barracks.

"The duke himself asked me not to share any details until they officially announce the news," I said, holding my hands up. My eyes flicked over to where Sorano watched from the golf cart Kai had delivered us in. They spoke in hushed voices, but Mandy's eyes lit as she caught bits of their conversation.

"My lips are sealed," she said, making a zipping motion in front of her mouth when she realized I was on to her.

"Great." Collins folded his arms. "Even more secrets for you two to keep."

"The duke asked *me* not to share, not Mandy." I stole another glance at Sorano. "Just wait till I'm in the barracks before filling him in. You'll draw less attention that way," I said as Kai leaned around the sergeant to give me another appraising frown.

Five weeks. How much more could they push me?

I left Mandy and Collins and headed for the harem. There was nowhere to stash a ball gown in the crypt, but I was betting Natalie would know what to do with it in the meantime.

A cacophony of excited voices echoed through the harem foyer when I entered. Andre and Blair had arrived ahead of me, and they'd clearly had opinions to share about the events of the night. Giggles and squeals filtered from every other door as the gossip made the rounds.

I found Natalie's door closed and knocked the chest of the glitter raven gatekeeper. When she didn't answer right away, I knocked again. I couldn't share what had happened with the queen, but I was excited to divulge my rendezvous with an anonymous, handsome half-sired.

The door cracked open an inch. I took the invitation and entered, wondering why Natalie was sitting around in the dark. Were she and Sampson trying to pull off another séance? A stiff arm shoved my back into the wall, and my blood vision lit the room instantly.

Natalie's bedspread was soaked. She lay in the middle of the mess, her vacant eyes staring at the ceiling, the side of her neck raw and ragged. Blood spattered the smooth half of her head and the collar of her jean vest.

"Natalie? Natalie!" I couldn't find my breath, and it had little to do with the arm pressing down on my collarbone.

Cain Davis sneered at me, the metallic glint of his imitation fangs caught my attention before he popped them out of his mouth and stuffed them into the pocket of his suit jacket.

"Perfect timing," he whispered against my cheek. I shoved his arm away, but he used my momentum to hurl me across the room, right onto Natalie's bed and her lifeless body. I scrambled to my feet and faced him.

"Why?" I cried, fearing I already knew the answer. Every breath ached with wrath.

Cain put a hand on the doorknob, but he paused to consider my question with a condescending smile. "I may not be Scarlett's any longer, but the bonds of lifeblood are not mandated by reason or decree. I will walk this half-life among her enemies, and I will make them suffer, destroy them from the shadows like I have done with you."

He threw the door open and took off down the hallway, taking long strides. His jacket and white hair trailed behind him, easy pickings for a takedown similar to Emma's. But I was too furious for all that.

I hit him like a train, taking us both to the hall floor in a tangle of knees and elbows. I grabbed a handful of his ghostly hair and ripped it out. Then I tore at the folds of his coat, trying to get to the meat of him, rage consuming my actions. He screamed up at me, but I cut him off with a sharp strike to the throat, immediately delivering another one to his solar plexus with my elbow.

Another scream echoed through the adjacent hallway, and Blair Hanson spilled out of a room, falling to her knees farther down on the same rug I had Cain pinned to. Her red hair was up in the French twist she'd worn to the party, and I could see her grief-stricken face clear as day.

Cain smirked and then let out a pathetic gasp. "Help! She's gone mad!" he screamed, thrashing beneath me. "She killed her donor!"

"What?" I snarled in his face. My fangs dug into my bottom lip as my teeth clenched.

Blair slammed into me. The force of her assault lifted me up off Cain, and my spine spasmed as it connected with the concrete wall. She held me there, inches off the ground, one arm across my throat, and pressed her face in close to mine.

"Did you kill Gavin, too? I know you wanted him," she said, a raw edge slipping into her voice. I gurgled around my crushed windpipe, unable to answer her.

The steel fangs I'd swiped from Cain's jacket were hot in my hand, still slick with Natalie's blood—Gavin's, too, I guessed. I pressed them into the side of Blair's throat, drawing a startled breath from her. My hand trembled, biting the metal tips in deeper, but that seemed to sharpen Blair's attention.

She slowly lowered me to the floor, her eyes dilated and fangs extended.

"These are Cain's," I rasped, holding them back for her to see.

"You're lying." Her lips peeled back, distorting her pretty features.

"He's been trying to get rid of me since I got here," I said. "And you know exactly why. Whose harem did you snatch him from, Blair?"

"Scarlett." she breathed the name, nearly choking on it. "But that was twenty years ago."

"They shared lifeblood."

"No." She shook her head, refusing to believe me. "First, you blamed Sonja on Mic, and now Cain—"

"Mic's being released." I ground my teeth, feeling my fangs bulge again. "Cain did this. He did it all. The coffin in the pool, the live round, Sonja."

Blair finally took her eyes off me long enough to cast a cynical glare over her shoulder. Cain held his hands up, the picture of innocence.

"Who are you going to believe? A rogue vampling, or a member of your own house?"

Blair's breath grew heavy as if she might begin crying any moment. A mewling noise slipped from her as she took an uneven step toward Cain. "I can… I can smell him on you." She gasped, coming to her own conclusion.

Cain saw it, too, but he wasn't fast enough. Blair raked her nails down the back of his jacket, tearing through fabric and flesh. The half-sired groaned as he struggled to get away from her, but her fist knotted in his hair and wrenched his head to one side.

She bit Cain's neck at the wrong angle, striking an artery, and a thick stream of blood painted the ceiling of the harem hallway. The few donors who had peeked out of their rooms to witness the commotion retreated with horrified screams. But Blair didn't let up. Not until she had drained him of every last drop.

Chapter Twenty

After the hell I'd been through, the remaining weeks in the bat cave were nothing to write home about. They were downright boring. And depressing.

Blair and I were both coffin-locked, but only for a day until base officials confirmed Cain's DNA on the imitation fangs and matched them to the impressions found on Natalie, Gavin, and Sonja. After that, the duke and House Hanson were notified, and training resumed.

The new rumor on base was that our whole session was cursed. Three dead, and three falsely coffin-locked. We grieved and trained with caution.

Sampson took over as my loaner harem coordinator. He even moved into Natalie's old room, insisting that she would have wanted that. I broke down and agreed to a séance in her honor, moving the little disc around the alphabet board until the gang was content that she was at peace. I still wasn't convinced, but watching Cain pay for what he'd done was therapeutic in its own horrific way.

Mic was reinstated three nights after the ball, after recovering from his week-long coffin-lock. I happily relinquished the record to him. He made a point to thank me, personally and publicly, for pressing the duke to release him. Blair did, too. Andre had never really given me much trouble, but even he became nicer in those last few weeks.

Without Cain to stir discord in the human unit, Collins had an easier time of things, too. Mandy was still pleased as Punch with her own program, especially after Carmichael invited her to come back and camp with the local pack anytime.

Graduation day arrived sooner than I expected, and with it, the promise of seeing Roman again. He took precedence over everything else on my plate, ranking above my quest to bring Scarlett to justice, the first holiday gathering I'd be sharing with my sister in over a decade, and even the ominous research Vin wanted to share with me—despite the fact that I'd broken up with him over the phone shortly after the ball.

The skewed nature of my priorities wasn't lost on me, and though I tried, there was no resolving the matter through common sense. Love—lust—whatever…was not a sensible emotion.

There wasn't a lot of pomp and circumstance to the BATC graduation. On the final Saturday of training, a few hours before sunrise, the sergeants lined up all the cadets in front of the cave pool, and Kai handed us each a sealed certificate and letter of recommendation. No one really needed the letter—surviving the bat cave was proof enough of one's ability—but it was procedure to turn it over to your new captain on your first official day with Blood Vice.

I didn't know what I'd expected, really, with a super-secret organization like Blood Vice. The duke didn't even make an appearance. I assumed it was simply because he was up to his eyeballs in scandal, attempting to figure out who was behind the queen's attack.

I felt like a coward and an asshole for not telling him right away. But I was a *breathing* cowardly asshole. That had to count for something.

During one of our last phone calls, Roman told me that Vanessa would be my new captain. I was torn on how to accept the news. On the one hand, I'd be spending a lot of time with Roman. On the other, Vanessa was Roman's potential sire. He was *hers,* no matter how loudly my heart cried *mine.* Though it was a relationship on paper and nothing more from what I'd seen.

Whatever it had been in the past wasn't my concern. I wouldn't be asking him to explain why they'd shared a room at the Cottage Crypt. Though, I did ask Collins to drive all the way through, not wanting to stop there again. He was happy to comply.

The nights were longer than they'd been when we made the drive out, and they'd continue to lengthen until Midwinter when I would begin the six-month countdown to my adoption. I wondered whom I would end up with. Sonja's grandsire, while intimidating, had seemed like the fair and kind type. Could I be happy with House Starling? Would I have to move to Michigan?

There were other houses that were less appealing, but I had to hope after saving the queen's life that she wouldn't stick me with an asshat. Roman's outburst had made me reconsider the pros and cons, but in the end, I was still glad the queen had agreed to it. I desperately wanted to belong.

Roman couldn't understand. He'd been affiliated with House Sorano for twenty years. He'd been half-sired for fifty. When he was finally turned, he'd be prepared and surrounded by a familiar support network. As much as I wanted to believe that he was enough to get me through this, I knew better.

When Collins' blue Toyota pulled up outside my house an hour before sunrise, Vin was waiting on the porch, bundled in a wool coat. Seeing his lime-green Beetle parked on the curb gave my return a melancholy air.

Collins honked his horn in farewell, and the Toyota sped off. He was eager to get home to Lazlo. And Mandy had chattered for half the drive about the holiday plans she and Serena were making for the upcoming Christmas break. I hadn't mentioned anything about Roman to them yet. I didn't even know where to begin.

"I'm not here to win you back," Vin said as Mandy and I

climbed the porch steps. The announcement caught me off guard.

"Hi, Vin." Mandy gave him a small wave from under the weight of her snack tote.

"Mandy." He nodded to her before turning back to me. "It's your blood, so you deserve to know," he continued as I unlocked the front door.

"Deserve to know what?"

"That it's gone."

I dropped my keys. "Wait. What? What do you mean…*gone?*"

"I have a pretty good idea where it is," Vin said, pushing his glasses up the bridge of his nose. "But if I ask the thieving doctor to give it back, he'll want to know where it came from. He could take this to court just for spite."

"Why would he take it to court? That doesn't make sense." I pushed the front door open and snatched up my keys, ushering Mandy in ahead of me.

"Jenna." Vin grabbed my arm as I stepped inside. "Your blood cures cancer. No"—he waved his other hand as if trying to erase his words—"your blood cures *everything.*"

"Yeah, even death." I stared at him, feeling less surprised than I imagined he had hoped I would be.

"If I could just get a little more, maybe I could recreate the study with something synthetic—"

"Not happening." I shook my head and moved to close the door, but Vin's hand caught it, holding it open a second longer.

"It will happen, Jenna," he snapped. "I'll find another vampire if I have to. I just thought you might like to be the one responsible for saving so many lives."

"I *will* be saving lives." I narrowed my eyes at him. "As a Blood Vice agent. And what you're suggesting is against the law—"

"What law?" He scoffed.

"Vampire law. The law I'm now sworn to uphold," I said. "If I find out that you're conducting any more experiments on vampire blood, I'll have to arrest you and turn you in to the high council." A sympathetic note found its way into my voice. "I really don't want to do that, Vin, but I will if you leave me no other choice."

Vin's look shifted from scorned outrage to sad defeat and then back. "Roman was here earlier," he said. "He's driven around the block twice in the last thirty minutes."

"I thought you weren't here to win me back," I said, lifting an eyebrow.

"I'm not." He let go of the door and rubbed his hands together before blowing into them. "You're selfish and arrogant and heartless. There's clearly nothing here worth winning back."

I slammed the door in his face.

"He had that coming," Mandy said from the threshold of the dining room. She'd already put together a sandwich stacked half a foot high. "It's so good to be home," she said around an enormous bite.

I inhaled the orange and vanilla scent of my mother's candles and sighed. "Yeah, it sure is."

Not ten minutes after Vin left, Roman arrived. We sat on my porch and attempted to contain ourselves as we discussed the predicament we were in.

"This will wear off eventually," Roman said, sounding less sure than his words suggested. I didn't bring up the fact that Cain was still hung up on Scarlett after twenty years. I was sure he'd read the report himself.

"And until then?" I asked. "What are we supposed to do?"

His eyes zeroed in on my mouth, and he swallowed. "I can think of a few things."

"That's helpful." I laughed, but my blood warmed anytime he looked at me that way. "How does this affect your half-sired status with Vanessa?"

Roman grimaced at the mention of her name. "We don't

tell her. We don't tell anyone. We let this run its course and move on."

"Is it so cut-and-dried for you?" I asked, feeling wounded by his callous approach. "What if I'm not interested in being your dirty little secret until you bore of me?"

"Then don't be," he said, clapping his hands together as he stood. "I'm happy to fight the forces of nature if you are."

"Are you?" I folded my arms around my knees and shivered as a cold breeze swept through my front yard. Fall had come and gone while I was away in Denver.

Roman stuffed his hands down into the pockets of his jeans. "No," he answered truthfully. "But I'm not really the marrying and settling down type." He gave me a sad grin. "If that's what you're looking for, maybe you should have kept the good doctor around."

"Shut up and sit down." I tugged on the hem of his coat. "Our lifeblood dilemma aside, tell me what to expect on Monday."

Roman sat and rubbed both hands over his face with a groan. "Not sure that subject's going to be any easier."

"Why's that?"

"The duke wants us to find Ursula."

"The estranged duchess? Scarlett and Raphael's sire?" I asked.

Roman nodded. "Rumor has it she killed her own sire

before going into hiding."

"So that's what happened to Morgan?"

He looked surprised. "Kai told me you put a dent in the base library. I didn't believe him."

"I read. When I have to." I made a face at him and nudged his arm with mine. The small bit of contact tightened my stomach. Roman stiffened beside me as if he'd felt it, too. Either direction this went, it was not going to be a cakewalk.

I cleared my throat and tried to focus on work. We were going after the vampire responsible for creating the one who had killed me. Responsible for creating the one who had killed Will. Responsible for the one who had abducted and turned Mandy against her will.

Part of me was already plotting her demise, recalling Kai's law class and if there had been mention of any loophole I might be able to shove her through. But a saner part of me remembered that being coffin-locked was a fate worse than death.

That's what I wanted for this one. That's what the law demanded. And if I were the one to bring her in, I'd get to look her in the eyes when they did it. She couldn't know that I was Raphael's scion. She couldn't know that Mandy had killed him. But she could know that I was the one responsible for bringing her to justice.

Maybe that would be enough. And who knew? Maybe it

would lead to an early promotion.

A vampling could dream.

Catch up with Jenna and company in…

BLOOD DOLLS

BLOOD VICE BOOK FOUR

Available Now!

Jenna thought becoming a Blood Vice agent would solve all her problems, but now she's sworn to solve House Lilith's problems, too. And there's no shortage of trouble when dealing with the most regal vampire family in the United States.

The duke's first assignment for Jenna and company is to locate Ursula, the estranged Duchess of House Lilith suspected of murdering her sire. It's a tall order—a wild bat chase, some might say—and the long hours with half-sired agent Roman Knight soon drive Jenna to distraction, and possible destruction. Lusting after another vampire's pending scion is a dangerous game, one with legal ramifications in Jenna's brave new underworld.

ACKNOWLEDGMENTS

I am no expert on guns, police, or hematology. I do a massive amount of research to keep my facts as accurate as possible, and when my research comes up dry, I find someone in the know. I owe a great deal of thanks to those I've badgered with obscure questions for the sake of writing more believable fiction. This round, I owe extra thanks to Dana Barrett for answering my random police questions, Lisa Medley for the bloody insight, and my husband who knows a thing or two about firearms (and who's also my inspiration for many of the fabricated names for the firearms and ammunitions within Blood Vice).

A great big thanks to: my critique group, the Four Horsemen of the Bookocalypse, who are always supportive, enlightening, and all around pretty awesome friends and writers: Kory M. Shrum, Monica La Porta, and Kathrine Pendleton; my sister, Justina Dodson, for being the lovely cover embodiment of Jenna Skye; Bam Shepherd for her keen peepers that catch rogue typos (all remaining errors are my own); THE Professor George Shelley, for his invaluable literary advice and friendship; and YOU for reading my books. I hope you enjoy reading them as much as I enjoy writing them for you. Thank you from the bottom of my heart!

Even though I've already mentioned my husband in the acknowledgements once, and even though this book (and every book in this series) is dedicated to him and our son, I owe him another shout-out. I don't know how I got so lucky. This guy stays up late to proofread, he helps me research weird things, he cheers me on when I'm behind deadline, he reminds me to eat and shower when my brain is running on fumes, and he handles all the "real world" stuff while I'm off playing with my imaginary friends. I honestly don't know what I'd do without him. He makes me want to be a better person. This book is as much his as it is mine.

ABOUT THE AUTHOR

USA Today bestselling fantasy author **Angela Roquet** is a great big weirdo. She lives in Missouri with her husband and son in a house stuffed with books, toys, skulls, owls, and glitter-speckled craft supplies. She's a member of SFWA and HWA, as well as the Four Horsemen of the Bookocalypse, her epic book critique group, where she's known as Death. When not swearing at the keyboard, she enjoys boating with her family at Lake of the Ozarks and reading books that raise eyebrows. You can find Angela online at
www.angelaroquet.com

If you enjoyed this book, please leave a review.
Your support and feedback are greatly appreciated!